ORIGIN

ANCIENT BLOOD: PREQUEL

NORA ASH

ABOUT THE AUTHOR

Nora Ash writes thrilling romance and sexy paranormal fantasy.

Visit her website to learn more about her upcoming books.

WWW.NORA-ASH.COM

ONE
WARIN

Circa 1200 - Brittania

The scent of burning huts and freshly spilled blood was sharp in Warin's nostrils as he lifted his head to roar his bloodlust out into the night.

Distant sounds of battle—the final efforts of the defenders before Death inevitably gripped them in His cold claws—and the crackling of many fires was the only response.

He looked down at his last opponent, into his blankly staring eyes turned to the stars, and sighed with satisfaction. The rush of battle receded with the slow pulse of his victim's lifeblood seeping out on the ground from the fist-sized hole in his chest.

The amount of blood he needed to feast on before the

rage settled was never consistent, the thrill of brutality far overshadowing his innate hunger, and this night had been no different. However, now that both his hunger and his need to kill had been sated, the restlessness that filled him with liquid fire demanded a different kind of quenching.

For his brother, finding a willing woman after a night of slaughter was all he needed to fulfill the primal desires that governed their kind with an iron fist.

For Warin, the urges were never that simple.

He licked the blood still dripping from his lips and raised his head to the sky, nostrils flaring as he searched for whatever his instincts demanded to ease the roiling darkness within him.

It had been more than two hundred years since he'd fled to the wilds with his brother, and an unmeasured amount of time before that since he'd lost his humanity— he knew the violent, gnawing *hunger* tearing at him from the inside never went away, no matter how completely he indulged it. And yet he still tried. He *had* to try. Every instinct in his powerful body screamed at him with the rushing force of a thousand waterfalls until he satisfied it.

When the sweet scent of a terrified female reached his twitching nostrils, Warin's eyebrows rose in surprise at his own desire.

Huh. Maybe Aleric's ways were finally starting to rub off on him.

It wasn't that Warin was unacquainted with the female body—far from it—but he usually found his pleasure in playing with his prey rather than simply fulfilling the base needs throbbing through his body.

Her scent came from somewhere north of the village, where the fires had yet to reach the thatched houses. He could smell other humans up there, undoubtedly the few women and children who had hidden from the attack, but their scents were hardly noteworthy. The only thing of interest, the only thing his mind could focus on, was *her* —the unlucky woman whose life would end in his hands this night.

Warin ran, too far gone on the sweet scent of the female to care if anyone noticed his inhuman speed. He needed her, needed to consume whatever it was that called so strongly to him *right now*.

She was inside a nearly intact stone building.

His nostrils flared as he stepped in through the half broken-off door, taking in the smells.

An array of dried herbs, soot, and the even stronger, deeper scent of the woman met his senses. This was her home—and she lived here alone. There was no scent of a man overpowering enough to indicate that a mate shared her home.

Warin glanced at the many bundles of dried herbs hanging from the ceiling, noting the sharp, medicinal undertone in their smell. She was the village healer.

"Come out, little mouse," he called into the quiet room in the tongue he knew was used on these shores. "You can't hide from me." He undid his sword belt and let it fall to the ground with a clatter. He didn't need weapons to kill humans, but it was part of the disguise that allowed him to blend in with the raiders. Being unarmed might make her believe he was less dangerous. He always did love when his prey came willingly.

There was no reply, but he could hear her heartbeat thundering in her chest and her desperate attempts at quieting her panting from the table she was hiding under. The scent of her fear was intoxicating.

Calmly and with measured steps, he stalked over to her hiding place. Her heartbeat nearly doubled at his proximity, and he fleetingly wondered how much longer it would be before it burst out of her chest. Then he dropped down to a crouch, his lips pulling into a wry smile as he finally laid eyes on the girl.

"*Boo.*"

She whimpered and curled up into a tighter ball, pressing herself as far away from him as she physically could, her frightened gaze locked on him.

Warin blinked. Twice.

She was...

He frowned, unable to take his eyes off hers. They were the exact same shade of green as the sea underneath the cliffs the small village was perched on, and something in their frightened depths reminded him of... His mind grasped for the connection, but to his annoyance, the root of their familiarity eluded him.

"Who are you?" he growled.

The girl jumped at the sound, her disturbing eyes darting to his blood-spattered lips. A fresh wave of her fear-tainted fragrance curled in his nostrils.

"T-Thea," she stuttered.

Warin frowned. *Thea.* He didn't know any Thea. Aleric had briefly amused himself with a Theodora some decades ago when they were venturing far south, but she had looked nothing like this pale human with her auburn hair and smattering of freckles. And those eyes... He would have remembered a woman with those eyes.

He inhaled deeply, trying to place her scent, but at no point in time had he encountered a human whose aroma sang to him like hers did.

No, despite the odd moment of recognition, he knew without a shadow of a doubt that he had never encountered this girl before. This *Thea.*

But that didn't lessen his desire for her.

"Look at me," he demanded.

Her sea-green eyes flashed back to his even as a small whimper pressed past her lips at his snarl.

The moment he held her gaze, Warin let his will seek to capture hers. He felt the familiar tug when his mind connected and reveled in the rush of power that went along with it. It didn't matter that her eyes made his insides twist in a not altogether pleasant way—she was a weak little human, and he would make her bend to his will like he did with all his prey, until she no longer made him feel so... *wrong*.

"Come out and play, little mouse," he purred, holding out a hand toward her.

To his utter astonishment, she merely curled into a smaller ball, fisting her shaking hands in her skirt as if pulling the fabric tighter around her body would make her safer.

Warin drew in a disbelieving breath. No one had *ever* resisted his Compulsion before. No one *could*—at least, no human.

"Are you a witch?" he asked, somewhat hesitant to voice his confusion. As dangerous as they could be under certain circumstances, he had never heard of resistance to a vampire's compulsion to be among their talents. And he had personally feasted on enough witch blood to prove as much.

"No, I'm no one! Please, please leave me be!" Her

voice carried a note of hysteria and her body had started to tremble.

All witches he had met had been haughty with confidence in their abilities—at least until his fangs punctured their skin. This wretched little thing exhibited none of the usual self-assurance of someone who was accustomed to power.

But if she wasn't a witch, then why was she resisting his Compulsion?

"Come here!" Warin reached out again, putting all his power behind the command.

Thea's only reaction was to whimper.

Puzzlement aside, the girl's lack of obedience wasn't sitting well with his need to soothe his ravening hunger. With an irritated growl he flipped the solid table over, exposing her.

"Come to me," he repeated, daring her to resist him with a narrowing of his eyes.

Thea breathed shallowly, quickly glancing from his face to the door, clearly calculating her chances of escaping—and arriving at the conclusion that she had no chance of making it.

Her tongue flicked out to moisten her dry lips, momentarily distracting his focus. "Are you going to hurt me?"

It was a ridiculous question. Even if she had yet to

understand *what* he was, she undoubtedly knew that a raider who had broken into her home was not there for anything pleasant. Warin stared into her wide eyes, feeling oddly hesitant about confirming her fears.

Normally, he delighted in his prey's terror and went to great lengths to ensure they knew they would die at his hands, even as they surrendered to his Compulsion. This time, something inside him resisted the idea of hurting her. He wanted... Warin frowned, not entirely sure what he wanted. His fangs and throbbing cock were still aching to be buried in her, but he didn't want her to look and smell so frightened while he indulged himself.

It was supremely frustrating.

As far back as his memories would allow him to recall, he had always known exactly what his instincts demanded of him and had reveled in following them, even as he knew they would never be satisfied. This time, everything was *different,* and he didn't understand why. He just knew that he didn't want this Thea to be scared of him.

"I won't hurt you," he said. "Come."

She moved then, though hesitantly. His eyes followed her as she slowly unfolded from her curled up position until she was on her feet, hands still clutching her skirt. She didn't come to him, but at least she wasn't cowering anymore.

"What do you want?" she asked. "If you really won't hurt me, what do you want from me? I don't have any valuables."

"You." The word flowed easily from his lips, loosening the coil of confusion in his chest. Yes, that was exactly what he wanted, no matter the confusing emotions swirling in his mind. It was the only thing that was truly clear to him. "I want you."

Thea squeaked and stumbled back against the wall when he surged forward, but he caught her easily around the waist before she could fall. Her skin was so warm against his. Warm and soft. Ignoring her panting breath and the rapid drumming of her heart, he bent his head to her neck and inhaled deeply.

Her scent filled his lungs, tainted by the tart notes of her fear, but still rich and irresistible like nothing else he had experienced. His fangs burst forth, lengthening with almost painful speed rather than their usual, slow descent, aching to be buried in her creamy neck.

Warin groaned and clutched her closer. *Yes, just a taste...*

He nibbled at her throat, savoring the salty taste of her skin and the sensation of her pulse against his lips, but when his fangs scraped against her neck, preparing to puncture her skin, a sudden, loud *thwack* followed by a mild stinging in his cheek made him pause, bewildered.

It took him two full seconds to realize that the girl had slapped him.

"Don't you dare! Demon!" Her voice was filled with more than just fear now. She was angry, he realized when he pulled his head back to look at her. Her face was blotchy and her eyes darkened with fury.

Without releasing his hold on her squirming form, he touched his cheek where her hand had connected with his face. Her puny, human strength had not been enough for the mild pain to linger, but the sheer audacity of the assault stunned him.

She had struck him. A human had *struck* him.

Anger swept over him, replacing the bewilderment. *No one* raised their hand to him and lived—not even this disconcerting little female.

When he growled deeply, displaying his fangs fully as the animal part of him took over, the fury in her gaze died, replaced by pure terror. In her eyes he saw his own reflection, saw the monster within him burst forth to claim her life as it had thousands before her.

Only this time, rather than the usual euphoria, its demand for blood brought him only pain.

CHAPTER 2

WARIN

"Why are you sitting here, sulking like a petulant child?"

His brother's lighthearted tone didn't make Warin look up from the green sea below the cliff he was perched on, dangling his feet over the abyss. The salty wind felt good against his face and masked the smell of burned wood and stale blood from the village behind him. He was in no mood to deal with a playful Aleric.

"Aw, didn't you find a playmate?" The tall, auburn-haired warrior flopped down easily by his side, ignoring Warin's warning growl. "I keep telling you, just eat the men and bed the women—keep it simple. As much as you enjoy your sick little games, a nice fuck is just as satisfying and quite a bit easier to come by."

Instead of the swift punishment he usually dealt out when his younger brother overstepped, Warin just pressed his lips tightly together and stared at the frothy emerald waves underneath them. A heavy press of something he hadn't felt in centuries was lodged inside his chest. *Despair.* Thick, gray, mind-numbing despair.

Aleric seemed to finally catch on to the absence of Warin's usual temper. Warin could sense the long-limbed man turn fully toward him, a worried noise making its way up his throat.

"Brother? What's wrong?"

There was no one other than Aleric—the only being still walking this Earth who truly knew him—who he would ever have allowed to see this moment of weakness.

"I'm a monster." His voice was as dull as the weight in his chest when he turned to look at the only true companion he had ever had.

Aleric blinked, surprise warring with the worried frown on his angular face. "Come again?"

"I'm a monster," he repeated, his voice flat and lifeless even to his own ears. "I am Death. Destruction."

At other times, his light-hearted brother might have made a quip, but the expression on Warin's face seemed to startle him enough to alter his usual tactics for dealing with his elder's often volatile moods. "You are a vampire, Warin," he said calmly. "Haven't you told me all these years that we live to please the beast within? You were the one who taught me to take pride in what I am. Now, tell me what has brought this foul mood upon you, my blood?"

Aleric wrapped his strong arm around Warin's shoulders, easing just a sliver of the heavy burden behind his ribs. Few of their kind were lucky enough to have such a bond with their Sire's other offspring—but then again, few had the dark history he shared with Aleric.

"There was a girl," he said softly, letting the wind carry his words away from his blood-smeared lips.

Aleric perked up, and Warin could see his nostrils twitch, undoubtedly searching for hints of sexual congress. His brother had a weakness for human females and the delights they offered. "Yeah?"

"She made me feel..." He grasped for the right words to describe exactly what Thea had made him feel and failed. *"Wrong,"* he finally settled on, scrunching up his nose at the inadequacy of the term. "So... *wrong.*"

"Wrong how? Was she pretty?"

Though Warin could see Aleric was doing his best to understand what he was talking about, he was not at all grasping the troubling unease the human girl had stirred deep in his very core. He snorted at the unimportant notion of her looks. "I care not about prettiness."

Aleric heaved a sigh next to him. "And that, my friend, is why you're sitting on a cliff, brooding, instead of delighting in what the village has to offer. Do we need to go south again? You seemed to enjoy feasting on Romans."

Warin scoffed. What he had enjoyed was killing priests, showing them that he was a much stronger power than the god they prayed to while he played with them. The memory instigated an unpleasant and unexpected twinge in that dark place behind his ribs. He rubbed at his chest and, for the first time since he had known about their existence, worried that vampires might fall ill. Perhaps he was sick?

The thought was troubling, and was followed by a host of thoughts and emotions he couldn't make sense of. *Great.* More confusion. He hated not understanding a problem. The few times he had met such an anomaly in the past, it had been easy enough to solve it by wreaking havoc upon whatever the root of it was. This time... he didn't even know how to figure out what the root was.

Warin collapsed onto his back and stared up at the starlit sky, feeling small and hollow and not at all like the powerful creature he had been for the past centuries. *Wrong.*

"Brother..." Aleric's voice was rough with concern. Warin couldn't blame him. If he didn't feel so empty, he'd be concerned too. This—whatever *this* was—was a far cry from the vampire who had saved them both from the clutches of their Sire and spent centuries feasting on human blood across the European continent. But even the ever-present beast inside of him was quiet now, curled up and aching.

"Warin," Aleric tried again. His auburn head appeared above Warin, blocking out his view of the night sky. "Do you need... an Ancient?"

The suggestion was so ridiculous that the despair in his chest withdrew enough for an incredulous snort to make its way up his lungs and out his nostrils. "I am not dying. I have no need for an Ancient's blood. And even if I did, how do you suggest we find one willing to trade his blood without demanding our lives in return? I would rather perish than be enslaved." *Again.*

The mere notion of submitting to an Ancient's will made the wounded beast in his chest rear its head with a snarl. *Never!*

"I would steal the blood, if need be. Just tell me what you require, brother, and I will bring it."

The devotion in the tall vampire's otherwise fierce face paired with his ludicrous words ignited a smile across Warin's tainted lips. He lifted a palm off the ground and cupped Aleric's strong jaw with it. "You will do no such thing. I value your companionship far too much to see you attempt to take on an Ancient. I will find an answer to this on my own."

Aleric frowned down at him, his blue eyes not

displaying any sort of conviction. "What is 'this'? I don't understand what's wrong with you. We have raided countless villages with this group of Vikings. But after this one... I find you like *this*. Is it a curse? Was the girl a witch?"

Maybe it was a curse. He felt relatively sure Thea wasn't a witch, but that didn't mean someone else couldn't have cast some form of protection over her house. Or her.

In either case, the answer would lie with her.

Warin sat up as a piece of the puzzle snapped into place. *She* was the root of this problem.

The insignificant human with her sea-green eyes was the key.

His beast growled in agreement, and an odd exhilaration traveled through his body in response. He cast a glance up at the sky and saw the first signs of the impending sunrise in the east as the dark black of night gave way to deep blue. Whatever fix there was to the problem, he wouldn't have time to execute it tonight. But tomorrow night, he would rise, and then he would *act*. And whatever *"this"* was, he knew the root of it now.

One way or the other, the dull ache in his chest would go away when he rose again.

Despite the still-looming pressure behind his ribs, he got to his feet in a single, smooth movement and looked up at his taller companion. "Let us go to ground. Tomorrow night will be better."

His brother watched him warily, clearly bewildered with the sudden change, but he followed him wordlessly as he darted for the nearby tree line to find a resting place.

CHAPTER 3
ALERIC

The fresh soil crumbled around Aleric's up-stretched hand as he broke through the surface and into the evening chill. His usual elation at waking up surrounded by the embrace of the Earth coursed through his veins, along with a pang of hunger. He pushed through to the dirt and jumped out of the makeshift grave he'd dug for the night, ready to run, fight, *hunt*.

Then his gaze fell on his brother, who had climbed out of his own grave moments before, and a sinking feeling nestled in his gut.

The dark-haired vampire was crouched on the ground, peering up at the stars as if lost in thought, his deceptively young face void of the usual ferocity that had marked his features in most of the years Aleric had known him.

Whatever it was that had possessed him the night before, it clearly hadn't passed.

"Good evening, brother," Aleric called, discreetly scenting the air for the taint of sorcery. There was none. If it was witchcraft, the trace of it was long gone. "How did you rest?"

Warin looked at him over his shoulder, an odd fire behind his blue eyes. "We will be leaving the raiders tonight. Feed quickly—we are traveling further inland."

Aleric blinked, a bit thrown off by his brother's odd shift in mood. Last night he'd been melancholic and almost frighteningly passive, and now he wanted to hurry along a feeding? It was usually the best part of the night for both of them. Aleric considered objecting, but changed his mind when Warin lifted his face back up to the sky and sat still, like a hunched sentinel. Whatever his brother needed him to do to get through this unsettling episode, he'd do. Even rush through a meal.

With a huff he set out toward the burned-down village to find the men they had raided with for the past couple of months. If there were no surviving villagers left, one of them would have to do for a quick feeding.

IT WAS ONLY after hours at breakneck pace through thick forests and across trickling streams and sweeping meadows that Aleric caught the scent of what his Elder was so determinedly chasing.

Soot and the tang of fear clung to the branches hanging over the narrow path, marking their prey as a runaway villager. The scent of woman underneath made Aleric narrow his eyes in suspicion. Warin had blabbed about some girl making him feel *wrong*. Given the single-minded focus he displayed as they ran through the forest, Aleric had a sinking feeling he'd soon get to see the female who'd bewitched his brother so.

She was close now. Droppings on the path and the smell of animal mingling with the human's fear told him she was riding, but no horse could ever outrun a vampire. Judging by the smell of sweat, she'd been riding since dawn, and they would be upon her soon.

How she was even alive in the first place, Aleric had no idea. His brother's bloodlust was as inescapable as it was gruesome. Sure, he might play with his food for a couple of hours, but in their more than two hundred years together, since the night they escaped their Sire, Warin had never let a human he'd set his sights on live to see daylight.

What was so special about this one?

Aleric's thoughts came to an abrupt halt when Warin

stopped and veered off into the underbrush and sank into a crouch, his gaze locked on something further ahead.

Aleric followed him. The sounds of crackling firewood and a faint orange glow told him as clearly as his brother's predatory prowl that they'd caught up to their prey. Curiosity burned in his veins as he sank down into a crouch next to Warin.

He arched an eyebrow at the sight of the woman who'd curled up by the small fire in the clearing ahead of them. She was dirty and exhausted-looking, with long, tangled hair and soot streaks across her face. Red rimmed her eyes and he could smell dried salt on her cheeks. She'd been crying probably all the way up until she became too dehydrated to continue.

All in all, she was a pretty pathetic sight. Pretty enough underneath all the grime, sure, but nothing special. Why had this particular girl caught his brother's attention?

Her horse, who'd been eagerly grazing at the meadow's lush vegetation, suddenly lifted its head, nostrils flaring. No doubt it had caught the scent of lurking predators. It let out a panicked whinny and reared up, pulling at the reins tying it to a broken tree stump with all the desperation of an herbivore knowing it was about to become dinner. Not that either vampire would ever touch an animal when there was a delectable little human nearby.

"Shh, shh, be still!" The girl got to her feet in an attempt to calm the animal, but her soothing words did little to calm the beast.

Warin chose that moment to stand up and deliberately put his foot on a dry branch. It snapped with a crack that rang through the clearing.

The girl spun around, fear plain on her face. Aleric could hear her heart thundering in her chest.

The horse used her distraction to tear free of her grip, finally breaking the reins that tied it to the tree stump. It reared back again with another whinny, spun around, and disappeared in the opposite direction at a full gallop.

"No!" the woman cried after her four-legged companion, but it was no use.

Silence fell over the clearing, save for the crackle of burning wood and her quick breaths. She scanned the tree line, eyes wide and fearful.

Warin took a slow, deliberate step forward, snapping another branch under his bare feet. The woman jolted at the sound and grasped a burning log from the fire, holding it out in front of herself like a weapon.

"Show yourself!" she demanded, her voice much stronger than her panicked heart would suggest.

Aleric caught the wry smile on Warin's lips as he stepped fully out into the clearing.

The gasp of recognition from the woman the second

she laid eyes on him cemented Aleric's hunch that this was, indeed, the same girl his brother had run into the night before.

"Stay away, demon!" she shouted, swinging the branch in front of her so the sparks flew like fireflies around her. "I am not afraid of you!"

Warin made an amused sound. "Your heart says otherwise, little bird. *Da-dum, da-dum, da-dum,* racing against your ribs so loudly I can hardly think." He spoke in her language, but his accent revealed the lingering touch of the northern lands they both hailed from. They had learned this island's language during their travels, amusing themselves with the carnage of battle when they joined a raiding party. They cared little for gold and treasure, but the *blood...*

For two hundred years they had wandered the European continent, seeking out human battles. They relished the fight and feasted on blood of friend and foe alike. It was their sole purpose: rise with the stars and hunt for blood until the beast within was sated yet another night.

"I hunger for you," Warin said, advancing on the girl. She took a step back, eyes locked on his form. "I *thirst.* Your heart calls to me. *Da-dum, da-dum, da-dum.* Why? What magic runs through your veins, little one?"

She backed up as he walked toward her, prowling like

a big forest cat, her gaze never leaving his. "I don't know what you are or what you want from me, but I promise you, I will never give you anything! Not a drop of my blood, nor my soul. Begone, monster!"

Warin pounced then, moving faster than her weak human eyes could follow. He was behind her in the blink of an eye, one strong hand wrapped around her wrists. Deftly, he ripped the makeshift torch from her and threw it back on the campfire, rendering her defenseless in his grasp.

Aleric grimaced. He'd seen his brother torment countless humans over the years. He himself had slaughtered thousands. They were food, after all—food and warm, soft bodies built to pleasure. But Warin's needs were far darker than his own, his beast's demands more sophisticated. It wasn't enough for him to feed and fuck, and the games he played with his hapless victims were unsettling, even by vampire standards.

Aleric hadn't know their Sire for long, and for that he would always be in Warin's debt. For the eighty-some years before Aleric had felt the Night's Embrace, Warin had been alone with their Sire.

Something had broken within him during that time.

Whatever this girl had done to attract Warin's attention, before the night was over she'd wish she had died by a raider's hand back in her shithole of a village.

"You smell... divine," Warin murmured as he drew his nose up along the side of her neck where her pulse drummed rapidly. Her shallow gasps made her chest heave and her pupils blew wide with terror. When Warin's fangs lengthened with a *snick*, she flinched and whimpered, but the vampire didn't let her escape. He kept her pressed tightly against his own body as he nuzzled her neck with his nose.

"Stop playing with your food," Aleric sighed as he stepped into the clearing. "I keep telling you, they taste better without the bitter notes of fear."

The woman in Warin's grip jerked and cried out at his appearance. She wouldn't be able to understand the language he'd spoken, but he knew she'd have no trouble recognizing him as another Nightwalker.

"I'm not playing," Warin sighed. His eyelids were half-closed as he sniffed and nudged at his prey, much like a loving cat. "She's magnificent, isn't she?"

Aleric arched an eyebrow at the pathetic human. She was small and dirty and scared witless, and for the life of him, he couldn't tell what had his brother so enthralled. But he knew better than to question his Elder when he was consumed by bloodlust.

"Wonderful," he said, his tone dry. "Are we staying here for the night then, or do you plan to be quick about it?"

Warin finally looked up from the girl's neck then, and something... *odd* seemed to flame in his eyes. He wasn't lost to bloodlust. No, this was... something else. Something deeply disturbing.

"I want to keep her."

"*Keep* her?" Aleric raised his eyebrows in disbelief. "You want to *Embrace* this pathetic human?!"

Warin growled. The girl flinched again and tears began to leak from her eyes, but Warin didn't pay her any mind. "I will *never* sire a Child. You know this." His furious expression softened as he pressed his cheek against the crying girl's. "She will stay human. And she will stay with me."

Aleric narrowed his eyes at the girl. She had to be some sort of witch to have made his brother lose his mind within the span of a single night. "And what, exactly, do you plan to do with your new pet?"

"You speak as if this is unheard of. We have encountered many of our kind who kept human companionship," Warin snarled, clearly irritated with Aleric's less than ecstatic response to this newest twist in their journey. He released the girl and stepped toward the taller man. "You yourself have pet humans whenever we stay in towns for any length of time. Why shouldn't I?"

Aleric resisted the urge to roll his eyes. Instead, he looked his brother up and down, arching an eyebrow as he tried to find a way of explaining his... hesitance... at the idea of Warin growing attached to a human he'd picked up in the middle of the wilderness. Preferably without getting the temperamental Elder in one of his *moods*. His long, dark hair stuck together in matted clumps. Dirt smeared most of his visible skin, giving him an eerie, wild appearance. Smears of dried blood still adorned his lips from their evening meal.

"Humans need shelter. Food. You can't keep her out here, and you dislike crowded towns. Just... put the pitiful thing out of her misery and let's continue our travels, brother. Maybe a trip back to Sicily? You did so enjoy the monasteries there."

"*No!*" Warin's roar echoed through the clearing, and Aleric quickly dropped to one knee in a show of submission.

"She is *mine!* She will stay with me." Warin pointed menacingly at Aleric, his darkened eyes narrowing. "Do not cross me! I have to know why her heart sings to me. I have to know, or I will go mad! I will not eat her. *You* will not eat her. As your Elder, I command it!"

Aleric blinked. It was the second time in his life he had heard this command. The first time had been when Warin had stood bathed in their Sire's blood, the wild flames in his eyes so similar to those now dancing in his gaze as he'd commanded his brother to never speak of what had transpired that night.

After their Sire's death, he was the eldest known vampire in their bloodline. His command was law. And yet, through their more than two hundred years together, this was only the second time Warin had used it.

And it was over a human.

Aleric bowed his head in acceptance, then looked back up. "As you command, brother."

Warin held his gaze for a moment longer, then nodded as well, some of the tension leaving his body. "She is special, Aleric. I intend to find out why."

Aleric got to his feet and glanced over Warin's shoulder at the girl currently sprinting across the clearing. She was still naïve enough to believe she could ever escape the vampire whose interest she'd piqued. "Then you should probably catch her, before she trips and breaks her neck."

Warin looked in the direction his prize had run off in, a frown marring his features. Aleric was pretty sure it was inspired by dawning realization that his new pet could easily die even without encountering vampire fangs.

He watched as the wild vampire who'd cared for him when he was still new and vulnerable bolted across the clearing and tackled the human girl to the ground, pinning her in the grass with a menacing growl. The same growl Warin had given him when he'd taught him how to survive and he'd done something unforgivably stupid that would undoubtedly have gotten him killed, had he been on his own.

The woman, whose face was currently less than three inches from Warin's bared fangs, looked like she was about to wet herself.

Aleric sighed and sank down in a crouch by her campfire to poke at the burning logs with a stick. Warin may have taught him how to survive as a creature of the night, but he had a feeling that he'd have to teach his feral brother how to live as a human, if this wasn't going to end in complete disaster.

CHAPTER 4

WARIN

"Be calm!" Warin glared at the trembling human underneath him. The smell of fear wafted off her in waves, and for some reason it was putting him on edge. Usually he loved that scent—loved every frantic heartbeat and panicked gasp for air as his prey took him in. On Thea, though...

"I said *calm!*" He pushed his will at her, felt the jolt up his spine as his mind connected with hers... and *nothing*. Again.

He glared at the still absolutely terrified woman. He'd never met a human he couldn't Compel. Until last night.

"Maybe it would help if you stopped shouting at the lass," Aleric drawled from the campfire. His voice was dry as tinder. "Unless you want to wash her in the creek, because I'm pretty sure she's seconds away from soiling herself."

Warin shot a glare over his shoulder, but his insolent brother wasn't even looking in his direction. Not that he'd need to, to know Thea was scared. Her heartbeat drummed against her ribs so loud it seemed to pulse through his own, unmoving chest.

Maybe Aleric was right—he did have much more experience with human company, after all. Up until now, Warin's interest in a human hadn't lasted more than a single night—and he'd enjoyed their terror.

With effort and a grimace, he quieted the rumble in his chest and retracted his aching fangs.

The woman did look maybe a fraction less terrified.

"Now what?" he asked, in Saxon, so she wouldn't understand.

"Depends what you want to do with her, I guess," was the bored answer.

What *did* he want to do with her? He looked down at Thea, mildly perplexed. When he'd arisen, it had been with one purpose: find her, and fix the aching feeling of *wrong* in his gut.

But now that he had her, other urges were rising to the surface. Many he didn't understand, but there was *one* he knew—and knew what to do about.

Thea gasped sharply when the hand not pinning her

wrists delved between her legs and wedged up under her skirt.

"No!" she snapped, some of the anger from before returning to her gaze. But the scent of fear also returned, and she began struggling as frantically as a fish on a line.

Huffing, Warin withdrew his hand. Had she been anyone else, he would have forced pleasure upon her until her body contradicted her *no's*, and then relished her broken sobs as her flesh betrayed her spirit.

But that harrowing smell of her terror clung to the roof of his mouth, dampening his mood for the pleasures a female could provide, if not his need.

"*No?*" he hissed, sitting back up to gain a bit of distance from her unsettling scent. He was still straddling her thighs, and the heat from her seeped into his cold flesh, ensuring his cock stayed hard and aching. "I spare your life and you deny me?"

"You slaughtered my people!" she spat back at him, struggling uselessly against his hold. "You burned my village! I will never yield to you, demon!"

Warin opened his mouth to deny her accusations, but stopped himself before he could. To her he was just another of the raiders who'd pillaged her home. Perhaps she even thought they were all *demons,* as she called him.

Though, to be fair, he *had* cut down his share of her people. Feasted on their blood.

"I never burned anything," he said. "And I spared you when I could easily have taken your life and everything that goes with it. What more do you want?"

"Let me go," she said, voice trembling though she steadied herself to look him straight in the eyes. "I want to leave."

Those green eyes... they were as mesmerizing now as they'd been in her hut. Something deep within them pulled on him so strongly he was certain he would lose himself in their depths. And yet the longer he looked, the more he wanted to.

"I will never let you go," he said softly. "Whatever spell you've woven to trap me so, it has worked. You will be with me always."

She didn't respond this time, just looked up at him with fear and hatred all too plain.

Sighing, he got to his feet and pulled her with him. He had to drag her by the arm to get her to return to the campfire where Aleric waited.

"You *could* just Compel her," his brother said when Warin had to force her to sit down next to him, hand clamped around her ankle to stop her from trying to run again. Aleric was right—humans were frail, and she could easily break her neck if she tried to run through the forest at night.

"*No.*"

"So what's the plan, then? Get the girl to fall heedlessly in love with you of her own volition? Follow you around like a faithful dog?"

Despite Aleric's obvious mocking, the beast in Warin's chest rose with a pleased snarl. *Yes.* Something like that sounded... almost right. Eagerly he twisted to look at his captive, and found his elation souring instantly at the hostile stare she leveled at him.

It dawned on him that in his maybe three hundred years on this Earth, he'd never taken the time to learn how to make someone like him. Fear him, yes. Respect him, often. *Like?*

Perhaps once upon a time, before the Night embraced him.

A full body shudder rattled through him as memories so vile they threatened to eviscerate his senses crept in at the edges of his consciousness.

No. He would never think of those years.

And the time that came before, when he was still human, didn't exist. He had never been anyone but the ferocious vampire who even Ancients were wary of.

"How?" He turned to Aleric without releasing his grip on the human woman. "How do I make her love me?"

The other vampire's eyebrows met his hairline. The question had no doubt taken him by surprise—mainly because this was the first time Warin had ever cared that anyone *liked* him, save Aleric himself. And their relationship was forged in the blood that flowed through their veins.

"What is it with this girl?" Aleric asked, his voice agitated now. "Why her? Why now? You've never shown interest in human companionship before. What is so special about this blood sack?!"

"I don't know! And I don't care. I *want* her. And I want her to want *me*. But I don't know how." He made an agitated gesture with his free hand. "She doesn't even want to mate!"

Aleric heaved a deep sigh as he looked to the girl, then back at Warin. "Fine. *Fine.* If this is what it will take to get you remotely civilized, I'll help. It would be fantastic to occasionally enter civilization without *someone* throwing a fit and slaughtering half the town before we've even had a chance to visit the local whorehouse."

"It happened *once*," Warin bit back, though the mirth dancing in his brother's eyes cooled his indignation at the accusation. "And if I recall correctly, you partook quite happily in that slaughter."

"It would have been a pity to let such a feast go to waste," Aleric said, a wry smile playing on his lips.

Warin sighed at the memory. That incident had caused them quite a bit of trouble with the Ancient ruling over the territory spanning that town. "So, you will help me win her favor?" he asked, eying his brother.

Aleric sighed again and made a vague gesture toward the creek trickling nearby. "Yes, I will help. You can start with taking a bath. You look like a feral beast—women don't often appreciate a roll in the hay with a man caked in dirt and dried blood. And do something about your hair, too."

IT TOOK LONGER than he'd anticipated to rinse the dried grime off his skin, and even though he'd spent a good twenty minutes working on his hair, it still hung down below his shoulder blades in matted ropes when he gave up and waded out of the water again.

What did it matter, anyway? How did his appearance have any bearing on what Thea thought of him? He didn't mind what *she* looked like—he would be as enthralled if she were covered in pockmarks and feces, because the throb of her heartbeat would still sing to him. And her eyes would still call to that achy *something* lodged in his chest where his heart had once drummed as rhythmically as hers.

Most likely, Aleric had just played a trick on him. The younger vampire had an apt sense of humor and an irritating tendency to let his mischief loose at the worst of times.

He also frequently nagged Warin about bathing more.

As irritated as Warin was with himself for falling so easily for his brother's game, he was equally as annoyed with Aleric for taking advantage of his distracted state of mind. He left his wet clothes to dry over a rock and returned to the campfire.

Thea sat opposite Aleric, keeping a wary eye on him. She hadn't tried to run again while Warin was preoccupied by the creek, which was good. He took it as a sign that she was starting to accept she had to stay with him.

"You can relax. My brother will not hurt you, either," Warin said in her native tongue as he came into the circle of light cast by the burning logs.

Thea jolted at his appearance—her dulled human senses hadn't picked up on his approach—and a small gasp escaped her.

For a moment, he took it as nothing more than her surprise... But then, as he was about to turn his attention to his brother and scold him for his cheap trick, Thea's eyes slid down his naked torso and blood rushed to her cheeks, coloring them a delicious shade of pink. When her gaze dipped below his navel, her tongue darted out to wet her lips. She was *scenting* him.

Even if it was only a subconscious reaction to long-forgotten, primitive instincts, Warin knew what that meant.

She desired him.

Heat rose like a firestorm in his gut and spread out through his limbs in a pleasurable wave. Aleric had been right—washing the dirt off his body so she could see it better had been smart.

There had been a long time when he'd hated his body for the pain it brought him, and even though those nights were long since past and buried in the darkness, Warin couldn't remember a time he had been pleased with someone admiring his physique.

Until tonight.

His cock stiffened, hard and thick between his thighs, but instead of being pleased that he was ready to satisfy her, Thea recoiled in horror and turned away as if the sight of his manhood repulsed her. As if she hadn't just looked at him with blatant desire.

Clenching his jaw at her sudden change in demeanor, Warin took a step toward her to force her to look at him again, but the sound of his brother's voice stopped him.

"Wait."

"For what?" Warin growled.

Aleric heaved a deep sigh. Warin had the distinct impression he wouldn't be the most patient teacher, but he was the only one available. And besides, he was the only one Warin would ever trust enough to admit his need for guidance. "She's still terrified. Look at her—she's not going to voluntarily spread her legs until she no longer sees you as a damn demon."

"I bathed!" Warin protested.

"Yes, that's great. You're now a clean demon. Now put her at ease—talk to her. Make her think your fangs are intriguing rather than dangerous."

Warin shot him a suspicious look at that last comment. Something he'd had to go over again and again when Aleric was still a youngling was the need for secrecy. They could never reveal what they were to any human they weren't going to drink. Frail as humans were, they numbered far too many for it to be safe for any information about the monsters who hunted them to spread.

"And just who have you been cajoling with your intriguing fangs, brother?" he asked him, eyebrow raised in challenge.

Aleric waved him off. "Unless you plan on Compelling that girl, you've got no hope of playing the Masquerade with her. She knows what you are—so if you want her to bed with you, she will need to understand there is more than a monster behind the fangs."

Warin paused, frowning. He'd never thought he *was* more than a monster. Aleric... Aleric was different. Even with this curse upon him, there was more within him.

He'd been a great Viking warrior when their Sire claimed him. A true prize for the bloodline. But as much as Warin had thanked the stars above for bestowing him with a blood brother as faithful and strong as Aleric, he cursed his Sire for dooming a spirit like Aleric's to the Eternal Night. He'd deserved so much more.

That was not Warin's fate. He knew his spirit was twisted beyond salvation. Even if he'd had a soul, it would've been sullied past the point of redemption long ago. He remembered the monster he'd seen reflected in Thea's eyes all too vividly.

It was all he'd ever been.

And up until last night, it was all he'd ever wanted to be.

So how could he ever hope to show her something that wasn't there?

"Just sit with her. Tell her your name. Ask her about her life," Aleric said, clearly taking pity on his Elder's deflated disposition. "But for Odin's sake, put some pants on first."

CHAPTER 5
WARIN

"My name is Warin."

The girl looked at him, eyes narrowed with mistrust as he sat down next to her. He was close enough to reach for her, and his palms ached to do so, but he resisted. Aleric was right—she didn't trust him, and so far forcing physical contact hadn't done anything to change that—quite the contrary.

"Not *'demon.'* Warin."

"But you are a demon." She said it as a statement, but there was a question in her eyes.

"No," he said. "Something else."

"What?"

"My kind has many names. Nightwalker... Cold One... Vampire."

"Cold One?" she asked.

Silently, he held out a hand toward her. Only after he closed his eyes, offering her the illusion of a measure of safety, did she gingerly touch her fingertips to his.

"You're freezing cold," she whispered, confusion and awe in her voice. "How can your heart beat when your flesh is as frozen as a dead man's?"

He opened his eyes, capturing her gaze. "My heart does not beat."

Shock and horror flittered across her face, but also… curiosity. Slowly, while keeping a wary eye on his face to ensure he wouldn't move, she placed her palm against his chest. It was so warm against his skin, and he could feel the faint drum of her pulse. It was like being touched by life itself.

She kept her hand against his chest for several long moments, waiting for the thud of a heart that hadn't beaten for centuries. When she finally gave up and pulled her hand away, her expression revealed more bewilderment than fear. "How are you alive? Are you a witch?"

He didn't take offense to her question, even if Aleric muttered a Saxon curse at her presumption. She'd lived all her life in a remote village—anything unexplainable would be presumed to be witchcraft.

"It may be magic that animates my body, but no. I am not a witch," he explained, keeping his voice gentle. Her curiosity seemed to dampen her fear of him just a little, and he found he liked it. For a moment, the glow of wonder in her eyes as she took in the magnitude of a man who could walk and talk without a heart beating in his chest seemed to win out.

Then her gaze fell on his mouth and a cloud of mistrust shadowed her face. She yanked her hand from his cool flesh as if she'd been burned. "You drink blood. I know what kind of magic flows through your veins. It is as black as your soul. If you live without a heart, then you must be a monster."

"I *am* a monster," he growled, his anger at her retreat surmounting his need not to scare her further. "I have slaughtered thousands more horribly than any human could ever replicate, and I feel nothing but elation at the memories of ripping flesh and snapping bones. Perhaps what gives me life is even the Satan you humans fear while you hide away in your churches and pray for salvation. It does not matter. Not to me, and not to you. You belong to *me* now, and you will give yourself to *me*—monster or no."

Rose splotches bloomed on her pretty face even as she paled to rival the moon above them—fury mixing with terror. He saw it in her eyes, too, that same fire that had sparked before she slapped him the night before. With his gaze he dared her to raise her hand against him once more, almost hoped she would so he would feel the sting of her temper and the bloom of her life force against his skin. But she didn't. Not this time. Instead, even though she was trembling so badly her words were jolted, she hissed, "I cannot stop you from doing to me what you want, monster, but know this: I will *never* be yours!"

The beast in his chest snarled at her words, wanting to *force* her to accept his claim. But the call of the approaching dawn made him push back the urge to show her exactly how powerful he was, how futile her desire was to resist him. Instead he stared her down as he got to his feet, letting her see every ounce of darkness within him. "You are *mine,* Thea. And you will be mine for the rest of eternity. The sooner you accept your fate, the less pain you will receive.

"Do not leave this clearing. I will return for you come nightfall. And then you will *yield!*"

CONSCIOUSNESS RETURNED moments after the last rays of sun disappeared below the horizon. The low pulse of energy from the soil surrounding Warin's still body seemed heavier this night—almost tangible. Or perhaps it was the energy inside him, drumming with the rhythm of a beating heart. Of *her* heart.

He lay still for a moment, letting the rhythm pulse

through him until it filled his body almost as if life had returned to his flesh. She might not be a witch, but she *was* magic. No mere human could have captured him so completely, mind and body. *Soul,* if he'd had one she could claim.

Eager to see her again, to hold her in his arms and smell her addictive scent, he pushed through the loose soil covering him and rose from the grave he'd dug after leaving Thea in the clearing nearby.

The night embraced him with its buffet of scents and sounds of the nocturnal forest animals. The beast within raised up, alert and ready to hunt.

He was hungry.

Thoughts of burying his fangs in Thea's creamy neck made his cock harden, and he hummed with pleasure at the thought of her warm body moving beneath his while he slaked his thirst with her crimson blood.

Yes.

Hopefully she'd had enough time while he slept to accept his claim.

Movement to his side alerted him to Aleric's awakening. He waited for his brother to push through the grave next to his, blue eyes sparking with the same thirst for life as they had every night for the past two centuries.

"I'm starving," he said the second he was free of the

ground, offering Warin a fangy grin. "Are you sharing your pet?"

Warin narrowed his eyes at the auburn-haired vampire, a possessive snarl rising in his throat. "She is *mine!*"

"Sure, whatever." Aleric raised both hands in surrender, but that didn't stop a huff from escaping him. "Guess I'll hunt. But this far away from civilization, it'll probably mean we'll sleep apart come dawn."

"Eat a deer," Warin said, his attention wavering as he pushed his preternatural senses toward the clearing. The only sounds of life seemed to be from a family of foxes and the rabbit they were hunting. "I want you close."

"Ew," Aleric said, a revolted grimace marring his clean features. "No fucking way. I'm not drinking animal blood while you feast on that feisty little human. If you want me to stay close, at least offer a wrist—"

"Shut up," Warin snapped.

"I'm just saying—I'm your brother. I'd offer you *my* pet." Aleric sulked.

"Shh! Listen." Tense, painful pressure built in Warin's gut, right below his ribcage. He pushed his fist against it, trying to ease the swirling sensation of intense dread.

"I can't hear a thing," Aleric said after a moment's silence. He frowned at Warin.

"Exactly," Warin muttered. He sprang forward, launching himself through the forest, not waiting for Aleric. The pressure below his ribs increased to the unbearable for every step. Why couldn't he hear her? What if something had happened while he slept?

What if she was...?

He stopped abruptly at the center of the clearing. The fox family had moved on upon his approach, dragging the rabbit carcass with them. The creek he'd bathed in the night before trickled merrily to the east. Wind rattled leaves on the tall trees surrounding him and carried with it only the scent of the forest.

She was gone.

"Well, that's what you get for refusing to use Compulsion." Aleric's pragmatic tone ripped him out of the sense of drowning. Warin stared at him, trying to make sense of what he was saying.

"Seriously, brother, I know you've not been one for using charm when a nice dose of fear will do the job, but if you're going to threaten a girl with rape and torture, maybe Compel her before you leave for the night." Aleric strolled over to the ashes left over from her campfire and kicked a charred log with the toes of his boot. "Looks like she left the second the sun cracked the horizon."

"I didn't threaten..." Warin's voice died when his own words echoed in the back of his mind. *The sooner you accept your fate, the less pain you will receive.* His Sire had spoken those same words to him so many times. Pain had always followed. Pain so severe, it had broken him from the inside out.

If he had been able to, he too would have fled from the wielder of that treacherous promise.

The pressure below his ribs sunk, turning to a hollow pit in the depths of his gut.

He'd spoken those words many times since he killed his Sire, to a multitude of people. So many of their faces blurred into a shapeless pink mass, the only distinguishable feature being a wide, open, wailing mouth.

Pain.

It was all he knew. Pain. Force. And the sadistic pleasure of imposing his will on the pitiful creatures he captured to sate the beast inside.

In a rush of clarity so sickeningly clear it made the pit in his gut ache, Warin knew why Thea had run.

She had run from him like he should have run from his Sire. Because she had seen him for what he truly was.

Monster.

He had told her himself. Told her those same words his Sire had told him. Over and over.

The blurry image of the thousands of souls he had tormented for his perverted pleasures flickered and faded until Thea danced for his mind's eye, screaming in agony.

The agony he had promised her if she resisted his will.

"Warin?" Aleric's voice seemed to come from far away. Worry marred his deep baritone. "If you didn't plan to hunt her, why didn't you Compel her? You must have known she would flee."

"I can't," he whispered. "I can't Compel her. I can't hurt her."

"What do you mean, you *can't?*"

"I have to find her." He pulled his mind back from the swirling vortex threatening to swallow his sanity and stared at the ground. Seconds later, he picked up her trail.

Warin ran.

CHAPTER 6
ALERIC

Something was wrong.

At first, when Aleric had seen his brother attempt to be civilized with the human girl, he'd thought that maybe this meant Warin was finally healing from the darkness brought on by their Sire. That maybe he was starting to lose the urge to maim and torture just for the fun of it, turning his attention to healthier pursuits—such as the warm, wet bliss between a woman's thighs.

But the expression on his Elder's face as he'd stood in the clearing in the woods, staring into nothingness... Aleric knew then. He wasn't healing. He was possessed.

Not like the stories that said a few very strong witches could possess a vampire. There wasn't magic around him —not that Aleric could detect, at least. But something...

something was wrong with his brother, and it had to do with the little blood sack he'd found in that cursed village they'd raided.

In Aleric's entire preternatural life, there had been one constant: Warin. Warin's strength, Warin's companionship... Warin's blood. The same blood that ran through his own veins and tied them together with a bond deeper than death itself. Warin had been his mentor when Aleric was too young to survive on his own, his Father in the absence of the monster who'd turned them both. And later, as Aleric came to mature into his new life, his blood brother. His friend.

He had known him for two hundred years, and this night, as he saw the horror and defeat cross the dark-haired vampire's features, Aleric knew he was no longer the same.

Something was wrong.

And it tied back to *her.*

As he followed his brother through the dark forest in a wild sprint, Aleric silently hoped they would find her dead. If she'd fallen into a ravine and snapped her neck, whatever magic she'd woven over his brother would be broken and he would be back to normal.

Or as normal as Warin got. But however feral his blood brother was, he had never scared Aleric more than he had tonight. That look of horror and defeat as he realized this Thea had run... *that* had scared Aleric more than anything that had come before.

"We're close," Warin said softly as he stopped by a tree. A single, long hair was stuck against the bark.

The dark-haired vampire caressed it absentmindedly as he sniffed the air. Eagerness bordering on desperation played across his features, making the sense of unease in Aleric's gut twist. What had that girl done to his brother?

And how?

Warin suddenly jerked, his fingers falling from the bark as wild, unadulterated fury mixed with absolute terror flittered across his face. Aleric smelled it in that same second.

Human males. Unwashed bodies. Dried blood. *Her* blood.

Aleric followed his brother as he burst through the underbrush so fast he hardly touched the ground.

A feminine scream. Rough laughter.

Warin roared, his rage echoing through the night.

The laughter stopped. Steel sang—a half-drawn dagger.

And then they were there—in the small camp between tall pine trees.

There were five men—bandits, from the looks of them.

Thea was on the ground next to the campfire, her wrists tied and blood scabbing on her temple.

They never stood a chance.

Aleric had seen his brother slaughter thousands over the years, all in gruesome ways. He had never seen him butcher with quite this much prejudice before.

Warin was a whirlwind of destruction, ripping off limbs and tearing out throats. Blood sprayed across the clearing, flinging chunks of still-quivering human flesh onto the soiled ground as the humans screamed in terror. Two of them tried to run. They didn't make it so much as a foot out of the camp before Warin ripped their spines from their bodies.

It was over in less than a minute.

Though the forest had rung with screams and howls only seconds before, silence fell over the camp when Warin tossed the final robber to the floor. Only Thea's gasping breaths and faint movement from the only man still halfway alive could be heard.

Warin retracted his fangs and sank down on his knees next to the girl. His face was a study in sorrow and regret as he gently cupped her cheek. "I am so sorry," he murmured. "Where are you hurt?"

Thea stared up at him—at his blood-covered lips and the obvious regret in his eyes. She looked like she didn't know if she was better off with her attackers gone and the feral vampire crouched over her.

"Just... my head," she finally said. "You came in time."

Warin brushed his fingers against her temple with a butterfly-light touch, his eyes zeroing in on the blood there. It wasn't bleeding anymore—the robbers had clearly only intended to stop her from fighting, rather than kill her.

"Don't run from me again." The words were the same ones he'd spoken the previous night, but this time, they came out as a plea, not a command. "I can't protect you during the daylight hours, and if you run, others can hurt you."

"Why would you want to protect me? You killed my people. You... you captured me." She sounded more confused than accusatory. Aleric didn't miss how she never looked away from Warin's blue gaze, as if something in it pulled on her. The same way her eyes seemed to pull on his brother.

"I don't know," Warin admitted. "But I do. I *need* to. I can't hurt you, Thea, and I never will. But I cannot be without you, either. Please. Don't run from me again."

"I don't understand," she whispered. "Who *are* you?"

Warin didn't answer her this time. He only folded the fingers not supporting her head around her hands, gaze locked on hers. The look of wonderment on his bloodstained face was clear, even from Aleric's perch by the dying man.

"YOU NEED to take her to an Ancient."

Warin's responding growl was fully expected, but Aleric held up a hand, stopping his Elder's temper from unfolding just yet.

"You need to know what she is, Warin. Why she's making you..." He grimaced and waved his hand. *"Feel* things."

"There is nothing wrong with her, or what she makes me feel," Warin said, voice low.

"I didn't say there was. But you cannot deny that she has changed you. That she influences you in some way that even you don't understand. She's not a regular human, you know that. We need to know *what* she is to..." Aleric hesitated for a brief second at the look of warning on Warin's face. "To make sure *she's* safe. An Ancient is our best hope of learning more about her and this... connection you have."

"And who's to say an Ancient will tell us the truth?" Warin asked as he glanced over his shoulder in the direction Thea had gone. She'd left the camp to bathe in the nearby pond, and the dark-haired vampire had been visibly on edge since she left his sight, even though they could both still hear her.

Aleric sighed. He knew his brother had an ingrained mistrust for the Ancients of their kind. The few vampires who reached the age of one thousand years were considered the ruling power in their fractured society. Each had their own territory where their word was law, and any vampire residing within would submit to their rule or die the Final Death. Their strength was insurmountable, and they'd often gathered more wisdom in their long life than could be found in any royal library across the continent.

Their Sire had been an Ancient.

"Why would an Ancient lie about the girl? The closest Ancient in these parts is the Night Lord of London. He has never even heard of us—he has no reason to trick us." Aleric gestured toward the bushes shielding the pond from their vision. "If we go to him, he is duty bound to offer his assistance. And we *need* his assistance, Warin. We don't know what this girl is or how she will affect you. We don't even know if she has the lifespan of a human, and since you don't wish to Embrace her... this twisted little romance of yours might come to an end someday."

There. He'd played his trump card. Given the way his brother acted at the scuffs the girl had obtained at the hands of those robbers, the prospect of her death was likely the only thing that would persuade him to do the smart thing.

From the look of begrudging defeat on Warin's face, Aleric knew his plan had worked.

"Fine. But we must be wary—you know an Ancient will never offer his help without a price."

CHAPTER 7
WARIN

The Night Lord of London may not have heard their names before, but he did know about their arrival in his territory.

From the moment they stepped foot on London's windy, cobbled streets, both Warin and Aleric knew they were being watched.

A short, lanky vampire followed them from the shadows, slipping behind barrels and dodging into narrow alleys as he trailed after them. He was barely a century old as far as Warin could tell, when he carefully tested the wisps of power radiating off the young man. Barely more than a child. He was no threat—which was why Warin knew he was there only as a lookout from someone more powerful.

"We should teach him not to spy on his Elders," Aleric mumbled in Saxon.

"He is undoubtedly the Lord's servant. We will do nothing," Warin warned, tightening his grip around Thea's waist. Every instinct in his preternatural body was on high alert—at the best of times, he hated the tight spaces and stench of human waste unique to bigger cities. This night, when he had a frail human to protect, he was in no mood to risk an Ancient's wrath because his brother was bored and spoiling for a fight.

Since the robbers, they'd both only fed on forest critters while making the journey south, and Aleric was in a foul mood as a result.

Warin glanced down at the girl by his side and couldn't hold back a small smile at her open-mouthed stare at everything they passed. She'd lived her entire life in that small village. Seeing a town like London was undoubtedly overwhelming. She didn't even resist his hold, seemingly content with the protection his presence next to her presented.

She still feared him—he knew that much, from the wary way she regarded him and how she flinched if he reached for her. But in the nights since he had slain her attackers and pledged to never harm her, she hadn't run, either. Every sunset when he rose, she was there. Waiting for him.

"We could still spook him," Aleric grumbled. "Or at least stop for a taste of the local cuisine." He eyed up a pretty whore batting her eyelashes at him from the doorway across the narrow street.

"Can we?" Thea asked, the excitement in her voice clear. What exactly Aleric meant by *"local cuisine"* seemed to have gone over her head.

"Are you hungry?" Warin said with a frown. He'd ensured she was well fed on their travel here, catching prey for her every night.

"Well, no, maybe not hungry, but..." Her gaze swept over the many buildings to Westminster, lingering on the impressive architecture for a moment before she looked back up at him. An unmistakable spark of the same excitement evident in her voice shone from her verdant eyes, before she bashfully lowered her eyelashes, a subtle rose coloring her cheeks.

Warin stared down at her. For just a moment, he'd gotten a glimmer of who she truly was. She'd been so overcome with curiosity of the city, she'd forgotten to fear him.

"Fine. Go find a snack," he told Aleric. "We will meet back here when the hour strikes midnight. Do not be tardy, and do not cause trouble."

"That's rich, coming from you," Aleric grumbled, in Saxon so Thea wouldn't understand his lip.

Warin narrowed his eyes at him, but Aleric pretended

not to notice. He cast a glance over his shoulder at their shadow and said, "I'll see if I can lure him my way—show the lad a good time, while you wander around town with your gawking human. Since my Elder is apparently determined to play lovesick fool with his pet."

"Is he angry?" Thea asked, drawing Warin's attention to her, rather than his obstinate brother. She'd apparently picked up on Aleric's discontent, if not his words.

"No." It wasn't anger Warin felt hum in their bond. Frustration, yes. And confusion. Even fear. He supposed it wasn't an odd response—Warin himself didn't understand why he was humoring the girl in her desire to see the town, when they had more important matters to attend. All he knew was that the excitement radiating off Thea in waves meant she forgot to keep her guard up for small bits of time as the wonders of the city seemed to overwhelm her. And Warin wanted more of that—more of her, without the shroud of unease she'd displayed since they met.

"Come," he said, holding out an arm to indicate the way to the river. "Let's see the city, then."

Thea spent most of their walk through the bustling streets of London with her mouth agape in wonder. Churches and buildings stretched toward the sky higher than even the trees surrounding her village, and when they stopped at the river to look at the massive bridge construction spanning halfway across the Thames, her eyes seemed alight with almost reverence.

"Humans have built all this? This city, and all these wonders?" she asked, not taking her eyes off the half-built bridge.

"Most of them."

"I never knew... there is so much out there, in the world, isn't there? So many things to see. So many people to meet." She looked up at him then, only a sliver of hesitance in her gaze. "How many places like this exist?"

"Countless. More still that have been lost to the ages." Warin touched her hair, pushing it away from her pretty face. "Do you wish to see them, Thea?"

"Oh, yes!" She seemed to realize what he was truly asking then, and bit her lip. Her teeth made small indents into the soft flesh. Warin found it impossible to look away. "I mean... I..."

"I can show you the world, Thea, if that is what you wish. I can show you wonders that will make this bridge look like nothing but a child's stick figurine." He spoke urgently, willing her to understand that he could give her so much more than what he had taken from her. "I can introduce you to kings and queens—I will *make* you a queen, if you so desire."

She looked at him, a frown drawing her eyebrows in.

"You speak as if it is so easy to bend the world to your will."

"It is." There was no point in lying—not to her. Even if his world scared her, he wouldn't hide the truth from her. Couldn't. "You have seen what I can do. You have seen my strength. Whatever you wish, I will give to you. If you follow me willingly."

He half expected her to screech at him, and call him a monster now that he had reminded her what he was capable of. But she only shook her head and looked back at the bridge. "What are the wonders of the world, and the people in it, if they are forced to surrender to my whims? You speak of strength, power, but it sounds so... lonely."

He stared at her in silence as London's inhabitants went about their nighttime errands. The last merchants were shouting from the nearby market, hawking their wares before they would return to their homes.

"I prefer solitude," he said, though he didn't know why. She hadn't asked.

Thea smiled, a soft curve to her lips he hadn't seen before. "No, you don't. You might be a creature of the night, but you crave companionship as much as any human. Why else travel with your brother? Why capture me?"

"You are *different,*" he said, an irritated growl to his voice that made her flinch. He hadn't meant to scare her, but her words unsettled him. He was nothing like the humans surrounding them in this overcrowded city, and nothing at all like the people whose blood he feasted on when the beast in his chest demanded sustenance. "Aleric is different."

"Can... can we go look at the market?" she asked, not challenging him, but not agreeing, either. When he went to wrap his arm around her midriff, she tensed, and he hated himself for having broken the small moment's truce between them. For a few minutes, they had been equal. Not master and captive. Vampire and human.

He brought her to the market that, even though the busiest time had long since past, still bustled with people and merchants.

Thea looked at it all with those emerald eyes wide open in awe, smelled spices from faraway lands and gasped at the beauty of jewelry, woodcarvings and tapestries alike. When she admired a comb adorned with shimmering pearls longer than the other trinkets, he purchased it for her with some of the robbers' coins and was rewarded with a shy smile in gratitude.

Aleric was right when he'd insisted they needed to come here. Thea was not human. But she was also not... *not* human. She smelled human, she felt human... she bled like a human. He had to learn more about her, if for no other reason than it would tell him how to best care for her.

And for how many years she would be with him before she aged and died.

A shudder rippled through him and straight to his marrow at the mere thought. Thea looked up at him, likely having felt him shiver, and he couldn't stop himself from reaching out and touching her cheek.

Soft. Smooth. Warm. He relished the contact with her skin until she pulled away with a jerk, as if startled she'd let him touch her. The deep blush spreading from her chest up her neck to cover her pretty face made his fangs ache.

She felt it too. He knew she felt that painful tug of longing behind the ribs too, had known since she let him care for her after her run-in with the robbers. She hadn't said it, of course—she didn't trust him enough for that—but he saw it in her eyes. That confused, pained, deep yearning.

And Warin had sworn to himself he wouldn't taste her before she invited him. Not her blood, nor the sweet heat between her thighs. As much as he ached for her, the thought of forcing her was too sickening. So, he would have to gain her trust, little by little, until finally, one day... she would give herself to him. Willingly.

THE NIGHT LORD of London spent his nights holding court deep in the catacombs of the most pompous church the city had to offer. If the parish knew what damned creatures haunted their sacred place during the night, they would likely burn it to the ground.

It wasn't an unusual setup for a vampire Lord—the splendor foisted upon a god's house, paired with the bitter irony that the most unholy creatures defiled these pitiful humans' sacred halls, was too tempting to resist.

It was never difficult to find an Ancient's residence. They allowed their power to light up the night like a beacon, letting every vampire in their territory know that these lands were ruled by someone far more powerful than the human king on his gilded throne.

The Ancient ruling the night in these parts was no different. Warin felt his presence grate against his own power, challenging the beast within. He suppressed it with a force of will as they descended into the bowels of the church. Even he was no match for an Ancient—especially not one this strong.

He held Thea tighter, reassuring her as much as himself with their shared closeness. The pathways were narrow, stone flooring turning to dirt, and soon he had to release his hold on her so she could move behind him.

Aleric took up the rear, his unusual quietude betraying his unease as well.

"You wish to see the Lord?" a sultry voice asked. A tall, beautiful woman stepped out from the shadows as they rounded a corner. She was wearing a deep red, silken dress, and jewels sparkled from around her neck and wrists. "State your name and your purpose, young ones."

Warin resisted the urge to growl at her haughty tone. She was older than them—he would estimate four hundred years or so—but he had not been called a youngling for two centuries. "Warin and Aleric Waldl-itch. We have come to ask your Lord for advice."

"Advice?" A small, joyless smile touched her lips. "Mayhap the Lord will be in the mood to part with some wisdom tonight. It has been a while since outlanders came to our town with the promise of intrigue." She tipped her head to look at Thea over his shoulder. "And you bring a present. How very thoughtful. Does she do anything? Sing? Dance?"

Warin's fangs descended without his consent. "She is *mine!*" he snarled, all thoughts of keeping his temper in check in this pit of treachery vanishing at the mere thought of these strangers touching his human.

"Oh. Another pet. How tedious," the woman said, neither her tone nor her voice changing despite the obvious threat emanating off Warin in thick waves. "I suppose we shall hope your request for our Lord will prove amusement enough. The nights run long when Zet holds court." She turned and walked ahead of them down the narrow pathway, leaving them to follow until a stone door blocked their way.

Once they caught up, she rapped her knuckles against the door in a light rhythm.

The hinges creaked with effort as the heavy door swung open, finally revealing the Lord of London's domicile.

The crypt was large, with a domed ceiling and several vampires scattered around the edges. Some were feeding, the sounds of human moans echoing around the sarcophagi, limp bodies and feasting vampires illuminated by torches.

And in the center of it all, the Ancient sat on the lid of a stone sarcophagus, a bored look on his deceptively youthful face.

"Verawein, you bring guests?" His voice rang through the room, stilling all within. Even the feeding vampires looked up at their Lord's voice.

"They come to ask for your wisdom, my lord," their guide said as she sashayed across the floor to stand by his side.

"Curious." He tilted his head as he took them in. Warin had to restrain himself from stepping to the side to shield Thea from his golden eyes as they roamed over her form, lingering for just a second at her neck. "It has been near on a month since we last had visitors from outside the territory. Come. Break up this tedious night for us and present your errand."

Warin walked forward, keeping a tight grip on Thea. He could hear her trying to swallow her whimpers and smell her fear as they passed by the humans who'd been fed upon, and pride swelled in his chest that she kept on walking. Most humans who hadn't been Compelled would have lost composure this deep into a vampire nest, but not his Thea. Not while he was with her.

"And what have we here?" Zet's nostrils flared when they stopped in front of him, Thea's scent undoubtedly hitting him fully. The Ancient leaned forward from his perch and reached out a hand toward her, his eyes narrowing. "Come here, child."

Thea whimpered in response and pressed closer to Warin, wide eyes glued to the Ancient.

Zet arched an eyebrow and looked at Warin. "If I am not mistaken, either you enjoy the scent of your pet's terror and have Compelled her to complete obedience despite awareness—an impressive feat for one so young as you—or... this human remains in control of her mind?"

"This is why we have sought your advice, my lord," Warin said. He fought back the urge to grab Thea and run until this suffocating catacomb and the powerful Ancient residing within was nothing but a faint memory, instead releasing his hold on her. "My human does not take to Compulsion."

An audible gasp from the court echoed throughout the room. Warin ignored them all and gently nudged Thea forward, despite her obvious reluctance. He had taken her into the bowels of London's night to learn what this Ancient might know for her sake, and for his own. He had to see it through. "She *smells* human, she *feels* human... but *something* about her isn't. I brought her here in hopes that your wisdom could shed light on what she is."

"What are you talking about? Of course I am human!" Thea hissed over her shoulder.

"How very curious." The Ancient's golden eyes returned to the young woman now standing directly in front of him. He curved his finger at her in a come-hither movement, full lips rising up in a small smile. "And brave enough to talk back to her Master, even when she reeks of fear. Come here, girl. Let me have a look at you."

Slowly, shooting Warin a pleading look, she walked the final few steps until she was within reach of the raven-haired Ancient.

He wrapped his hand around her jaw, and she shuddered at the contact, but didn't pull away. Though she was trembling, she returned his unblinking gaze.

"Take off your clothes, little one," Zet purred, his voice silken persuasion and molten heat. The strength of his Compulsion was nearly tangible, even from Warin's distance.

"What? No!" Thea jerked back from Zet's grip, crossing her arms over her chest.

The look of astonishment on the Ancient's face was quickly wiped away by sheer intrigue. He jumped off his makeshift throne to circle the still-trembling woman, eyes dark and predatory. Warin clenched his fists until his nails drew blood from his palms to keep from launching himself in between them and push the powerful being away from her.

"You *smell* human," Zet said, drawing in a deep breath. "You *look* human."

"I *am* human!" she said. "Please, I don't know what this is about."

"It's about you being a very, *very* interesting young lady." The purr was back in Zet's voice. "Is there anything else you have noticed about her?" The last part was directed at Warin, though Zet's eyes still didn't leave her. "She speaks the language of my territory. Where did you find her?"

"Far north, in a village on the coast. Well outside your

border, *my lord.*" Warin narrowed his eyes at the Ancient's back. Even someone with his power had to abide by their ancient laws. He would not be able to take Thea away by any obvious means, but his interest in her was unsettling Warin's beast.

"Her heart calls to me. She was mine from the moment I saw her, and she will be mine until the day she dies."

"Her heart calls to you?" Zet ignored his subtle claim, finally turning around to look at Warin. "How?"

"It..." Warin frowned, trying to find the words to describe what had him so bound to this woman. "It is like she ties me to the world," he said slowly. "When I saw her, I knew she was supposed to be mine. Her heartbeat is a song, pulling on me. *Calling.*"

Zet stared at him for two long, silent seconds. Then he snapped his fingers and turned to face the gathered vampires. "I am retiring for the night. Go, enjoy my town. You are all much too young to waste away in this crypt night after night."

From the looks his court shot at each other, this was not usual behavior from their lord, but it only took them seconds to obey this unexpected but obviously welcome order. Within moments, there were only two half-dead humans and Verawein left in the room, besides the Ancient and themselves.

Warin bowed his head and reached for Thea. "I thank you for your time, my lord. We will be on our way."

"Not so hasty, young one." Zet gave him a small smile before he turned to the female vampire by his side. "My dear, my orders include you too. I wish to be alone with our guests."

"But my lord—"

Zet lifted two fingers, silencing her with an arched eyebrow. Meekly, she bowed her head. "Yes, my lord."

He watched her as she left, closing the heavy stone door behind her. Once her footfalls could no longer be heard, Zet turned to the farthest, darkest corner of the crypt. "Come. There is someone I would like you to meet."

Warin exchanged a glance with Aleric before he put a hand on Thea's lower back and followed the Ancient.

Zet pushed a heavy stone sarcophagus aside that would have caused even Warin trouble, revealing a jagged hole behind it. And, just as he slipped through it, the power radiating off him like a lighthouse in the night dampened. Warin could still feel his strength, but he was no longer projecting it outward as he had been. Apparently, the Lord wasn't interested in attracting any of his loyal subjects' attention for whatever it was he planned to show them.

CHAPTER 8
WARIN

Zet led them through the narrow tunnel until it opened up into the basement of what turned out to be the cellar of a busy inn. It was hidden behind a false bit of wall.

"I've Compelled the innkeeper and the maids," Zet explained as they made their way through rowdy drunks and busty barmaids that had Aleric sending their exposed necks longing looks. "They never ask questions about the room I rent here, nor its occupant."

"And who's the occupant?" Aleric asked. A glare from Warin made him tack on, "My lord?"

"You'll see," Zet said. "Patience is a virtue, young one."

Aleric made a rude noise. "Sorry, *my lord*, I just think it's pretty fucking weird how you dismissed your entire court to take two strangers through your secret getaway tunnel to meet some mysterious inn-dweller. I'd like to know what we're getting into."

"Aleric!" Warin snapped, but Zet waved him off, an amused smile playing across his full lips.

"I like your fearlessness, youngling," was all he said before he turned back around and led them up the stairs to the rooms above.

They all followed, Thea clinging to Warin's arm as he shot daggers at his brother. Aleric pretended not to notice.

The room the Ancient rented was located at the very end of the hall, as far away from prying eyes as possible. He pulled a chain over his head that his shirt had hidden from view and thrust the key attached to it into the lock, letting it slide open. It was dark inside, but the faint smell of magic drifting out was unmistakable.

Warin narrowed his eyes at the Ancient. "It would appear my brother was correct in his brash assumptions. What is this?"

"Not what it seems, I promise you that." Zet pointed a single finger at Thea. "If you wish to learn what she truly is, the answer lies in here. Do you care enough about your human to push aside your prejudice, young warrior?"

"Warin," Aleric warned. He put his hand on Warin's shoulder in a silent plea for caution. He was right—this Ancient required caution, to be sure. No vampire would ever have anything to do with magic of

the sort this room smelled of without nefarious moti-
vations.

But...

Warin looked down at Thea. He'd come this far.

Steeling himself, he let go of her and stepped inside
the room, ensuring that whatever—or whoever—was
inside, they wouldn't be able to get to her without going
through him first.

A woman lay curled up on the bed in the dark. She
was breathing steadily. The stench of magic oozed
from her.

"*A witch!*" Aleric hissed behind him. The *snick* of his
fangs' descent sang through the air.

The sound seemed to stir the woman. She murmured
sluggishly, as if drugged, pushing at the covers on the bed
to sit upright. She waved her hand with a lax movement
and the candles on the window ledge and on the desk
lit up.

Thea gasped behind him.

"Zet," the witch murmured, seemingly blind to
anyone but the dark-haired vampire. "I thirst."

"I know, my dove." The Ancient walked to the bed
and gracefully sank down next to her. He brushed a hand
through her messy hair and touched her chin with a
finger. Then he extended his fangs and brought the same
finger to one sharp point, piercing his skin. A crimson

drop of ancient blood pearled on his fingertip. He brought it to the witch's lips and smiled wryly when she licked it off with fevered desperation. When she tried to clasp onto his wrist to suck at his finger, he gave her a sharp look that had her withdrawing with a jerk.

Warin stared at the witch, whose lips were still red from the single drop of blood.

There were many rules in their society, created to ensure the survival of their kind. The first, the most important among them, was to never, *ever,* let a witch drink vampire blood.

And yet this Ancient... this powerful being chosen to rule over others and uphold the laws of old... He fed his sacred blood... to a *witch.*

"You are horrified," Zet said. His face was passive as he looked at Warin. "No doubt your Sire taught you the gruesome tales of vampires of Old, who shared their blood with witches. Of how the witches grew so powerful they could possess our immortal flesh, and we were nearly made extinct in the Great Witch War?"

Warin nodded once, not taking his eyes off the Ancient. Thea was breathing quick, shallow breaths behind him—even if she didn't know their laws, she was picking up on the danger in the room with ease.

"Then he was a fool." Zet's lips curved up into the ghost of a smile. "Your blood is your power, young one.

Chain a witch with your Compulsion and feed her your blood until she is addicted..." He touched his now healed fingertip to the witch's chin. "...and you have yourself a very powerful ally. Isn't that right, Marie? The Great Witch War was started by an idiotic fool too young to Compel a strong witch. I am no youngling. And I am no fool.

"I brought you here because I believe I know what your little human truly is—but only a witch will be able to tell you for certain. So... the choice is yours, young one. Will you let Marie taste your blood to truly understand the human whose heart sings to you?

"Or will you see her wither and die with age without ever fully knowing what she is? *Who* she is?"

"Warin, this is nonsense," Thea whispered behind him. She touched his back—the lightest brush still fraught with hesitance—but she reached for him nonetheless. "There is nothing to learn—I am human. I am *Thea*. Please, let's leave. I'll... I'll follow you willingly."

And that was precisely why he couldn't.

That something between them—the song in her heart and the roar in his veins that drew him to her also touched her. He could never leave here when the answer was this close, because he knew—in the depths of his being and the blood in his veins, he *knew*...

Warin stepped forward and let his fangs descend.

Without taking his eyes off the witch, he bit into his wrist and stretched his arm out in offering.

She latched on like a starving wolf, her lips forming a tight seal around the wound. The erotic sensation of his blood being sucked from his body first surprised him—and then repulsed him.

Growling, he shoved the witch away with a hand on her forehead.

She looked at him with a faraway expression in her dark eyes, blood still dripping from her lips. *His* blood. "What is your question, vampire?"

"What is she to me?" He pointed at Thea with his unwounded arm. "What is she?"

The witch looked at his human and held out her hand in invitation.

Slowly, as if resistant but too curious to deny the request after all, Thea walked to his side and put her hand gingerly into the witch's upturned palm.

Marie placed her other hand on top of Thea's and closed her eyes. The stench of magic increased, and something *dark* seemed to pass between the two women.

"Do not interrupt them," Zet warned before Warin could move to rip his human away. His tone allowed for no argument. "You have my word your human will not be harmed here tonight. Let the witch do what you asked of her."

It mercifully only lasted a few moments. The second the witch released her grip on Thea's hand, Warin wrapped her in his arms and pulled her away, anxious to put his own body between her and the threat of magic.

Marie slowly opened her eyes, but when she did, there was no longer a faraway look in them. They were crystal clear and filled with hatred and fear.

"What is she, Marie?" Zet asked, his voice cracking like thunder.

"*No!*" She bared her teeth at her Master, defiance flaring in her darkened eyes. "No, you cannot make me! I will not break my sacred vows!"

"*Tell him*, witch! I command you," Zet snarled.

Marie let out a pained howl and ripped at her hair, but despite her magic, even she could not fight against the command of Compulsion.

"She is your soulmate," she said, face twisted with revulsion. "She is your salvation. If you bond with her, you will never be who you were again. She is the light that was snuffed out the day Death Embraced you. She is doomed to love you, and she is fated to betray her sisters to stand by your side.

"That is what she is, vampire. And if she values the light that still flickers in this world, she will end her life before you can use her against her own sisters."

CHAPTER 9

THEA

"That... that can't be true. She's lying," Thea croaked as she stared at Warin. He looked dumbfounded.

"She can't lie under my influence," Zet—the scary one with the dark hair and golden eyes—said. He looked at her with his head cocked, as if he were a cat and Thea a particularly interesting mouse. "And she confirmed my suspicions. What your Master told me sounded too similar to the old stories to be a coincidence." His disturbing gaze shifted to Warin. "You have been granted a gift unlike any other bestowed upon our kind. Why, I cannot tell you."

"How long will she live?" Warin asked, his usually so confident voice betraying something sounding an awful lot like fear.

Zet lifted his eyebrows in surprise. "I do not know if

her lifespan is different from a regular human's, but I cannot see it mattering. Surely, you will wish to Embrace her?"

"*Never,*" Warin hissed. "I will never damn another, let alone my... my soulmate."

An incredulous look lingered on Zet's face for a moment before he shrugged. "I suppose others of our kind may know more about this phenomenon. They might be able to tell you how long she may live without the Embrace."

"Do you know where I might start my search?" Warin asked, unconsciously grasping her waist and tugging her closer. He'd done that a lot since they entered London, and much to her surprise—and confusion—she found she didn't mind. She *should* mind, she knew she should. This was the same creature who'd slaughtered her village and hunted her through the forest to lay claim to her like some kind of a... a *pet.*

And yet... it felt... *safe.*

Thea frowned. Nothing about this... this *monster* should feel safe. He was dangerous—she'd seen what he was. His achingly handsome face and blazing blue eyes couldn't erase the horrors he was capable of.

But... he'd also saved her.

She had run from him, certain that any other fate would be better than staying with him. When she'd first seen the bandits in the forest, she'd been so relieved. Other humans. Help.

She bit the inside of her cheek at the memory of their rough hands and salacious threats. Warin had come for her, his monstrous wrath not aimed at her, but the humans who wanted to hurt her. He'd saved her from her own kind.

"I first heard of this phenomenon from the Lady of Rome," Zet said, breaking Thea's swirling thoughts. "Perhaps your search for answers should begin in Italy."

Warin nodded. "I know of the Lady Elyse. We will begin our travels south tomorrow night. I thank you for your time and your answers, ancient one. We will retire for the night."

Zet and his witch watched them as Warin led her back toward the door, but when Aleric—Warin's auburn-haired travel companion—made to follow, Zet said, "Stay, young one. Leave your Elder to his human for the night. London has much to offer, and I sense I would enjoy a night in your company. Your lip is most refreshing."

Aleric exchanged a glance with Warin, who nodded almost imperceptibly.

"Well, I wouldn't say no to a taste of witch blood," Aleric drawled as Warin closed the door to the disturbing room behind them.

Thea looked back at the now closed door while Warin

led her down the hallway. As any God-fearing Christian would, she'd been raised to fear witchcraft, but she still felt a pang of empathy for the woman trapped in the room with two vampires. Ever since Warin had cornered her in her hut back home, she'd feared his fangs. But he hadn't bitten her, despite his obvious urge to bury those razor-sharp daggers in her neck.

She feared the witch would not be so lucky tonight.

They walked down the narrow streets of London, safe from the night's rowdy drunks and lurking dangers on the arm of the monster who'd chosen her as his.

Her soulmate.

She had never heard that expression before, but it resonated through her like a church bell.

Soulmate.

Thea looked up at her silent protector—her kidnapper and savior. Yes, she had recognized him the first time she saw him, even though she was certain she'd never seen him before. Recognized something buried deep within those startling blue eyes of his. It was that same thing that had kept her from running again, after he'd saved her from the robbers. That delicate, beautiful *something* that seemed to tie the deepest parts of her to him, pulling her toward him even if she knew she should do anything she could to flee.

Was it his soul?

Did monsters even have souls?

He led her to an inn several streets away from where Zet kept his witch captive, and paid the innkeeper with coin taken from the robbers' corpses. He asked for wine and food to be brought to the room, even though she'd already eaten the leftover rabbit he'd caught for her the previous night before they entered the city, but didn't spare her so much as a glance. Instead he took up vigil by the small window in what she supposed was now their shared room, staring out into the night with a deep frown marring his pale features.

Silence fell over the room, and Thea wasn't sure what to do. So far, he had initiated all their interactions, but now—when it seemed they most certainly had something to discuss—he was silent.

Thea took a deep breath, steeling herself to voluntarily draw the vampire's attention to her for the first time, but before she could speak, a knock on the door announced the arrival of her supper.

She thanked the serving girl, not oblivious to the hidden looks she shot at Warin while she set up the food and drink, and felt a small measure of relief when the other woman left again. If she'd met Warin under different circumstances, she too would have been enamored by his beautiful face. When his fangs were hidden, he looked the part of a handsome young man from a faraway land in his animal skin trousers and roped hair. Thea had never seen anyone like him, nor anyone with features so angelic. It was bitter irony, or perhaps by design, that what hid beneath his so attractive appearance was anything but divine. Maybe his looks were so appealing to allow his prey to be lured to him.

She watched his profile lit up by the moonlight filtering through the window as she ate. He seemed lost in thought and didn't look at her once while she ate, nor when the serving girl returned to clear up after her meal.

"Is this why you haven't killed me?" She hadn't meant to ask, but the words slipped out before she could stop them.

Warin finally turned his head to look at her. His blue gaze seemed to glow from the moonlight, enhancing his supernatural appearance.

"Yes," he said. It was such a simple answer, but it held so much truth. *Yes,* he had planned to murder her the night they met. She would have been just another corpse on an unending list of people he had killed. And the only reason she wasn't...

"How can this be? How can we be..." Thea drew in a deep breath, forcing her voice to steady. "*Soulmates?* We are not even the same species. You... you *eat* people."

"I do not know," he said, his glowing eyes fixated on

her face. "But I know the truth in the witch's words. You belong with me."

"I..." She paused, unsure of what to say. As much as sanity demanded she refuse his claim, she couldn't. Not when the truth of his words sang through her blood. She did belong with him—she belonged to a monster.

What did that make her?

Was this her punishment for those nights she'd snuck out to gather herbs under the full moon? The village priest had never trusted her, and in the depths of her soul, she'd known he had reason to. She was no witch, as he suspected, but she had felt the Earth's magic flow through her bare feet on those nights.

And now, her soul was tied to a creature of the dark.

"Will you hurt me?" she asked.

The flash of vehemence in his eyes made her stumble a step backward.

"*Never!*" Warin snarled, his lips pulled back in either anger or disgust. But when he saw the fear on her face, his shoulders slumped and his pale features smoothed into grim acceptance. "I know I am... frightening. A monster. But I will never hurt you. I cannot."

Slowly— so as not to frighten her, she thought—he walked across the floor until he towered over her. She didn't move when he reached out to cup her cheek in his cool hand.

"I have been a monster for centuries. But for you, my Thea, I will become something else. I will always be a vampire, but I..." He paused, hesitance flickering in his gaze as he peered into her eyes. "I will find a way of chaining the beast for you. You are... everything to me."

"You don't even know me," she whispered, but even as the words flowed from her lips, she knew it wasn't true. He knew her better than anyone ever could. In his touch she felt their connection hum with an urgency she couldn't deny.

She knew him, too.

Her soulmate. Her monster.

Slowly, as if he was trying to resist the nearly magnetic pull between them, he bent his head down toward her. She raised her lips to his, drawn in by the same force.

His kiss was hesitant—a cool brush of soft lips against her own, trembling mouth. When she didn't pull back after that first, light kiss, he pressed against her again, so achingly gentle she would have never believed this was the same man who could rip people to shreds with his bare hands, had she not seen it with her own eyes.

Thea closed her eyes and kissed him back with all the anger and confusion and fear she'd felt since she saw her village burned to the ground what felt like so long ago. His soft lips parted for hers, a low growl escaping him at her aggression. Strong hands slipped around her hips and jerked her tight against his hard body. She moaned into his mouth at the sudden sensation of his muscles against her, suddenly no longer seeming a threat as much as a promise. Her hands roamed up his bare chest of their own accord, earning her another growl. His muscles tensed under her exploration, but despite the hardness of his form, his skin was soft to the touch.

When her fingertips dipped to his navel, the proof he'd been born by a mother rather than created by a devil, Warin's growl rose to a snarl. He clutched the fabric of her tunic, and with a speed that shouldn't have been possible, he ripped the garment up over her head and clean off her body. Her long dress followed, until she was left in nothing but her linen underwear.

Warin made a noise deep in his chest, a rumbling sound different from his growls. It made the small hairs on her body stand on end and goosebumps break out on her exposed flesh.

The vampire pulled back from their kiss, his blue gaze roaming hungrily over her body.

"You are... beautiful." His voice was filled with such wonder, it made a blush rise from her chest. She'd lain with men before, but none who had looked at her with so much reverence.

None who had been her soulmate.

Thea held his gaze as she slipped out of her undergarments until she stood truly bared before him. Her nipples hardened under his attention, her shallow breaths making her breasts swell in quick waves.

The tension in the air between them had her trembling, even if any lingering fear for the dark creature in front of her was quickly evaporating from the hot rush of yearning burgeoning between her thighs.

Warin made the rumbly sound again, the one that made her body vibrate with energy—and then he moved, faster than she could follow. He shoved her none too gently, sending her flying back on the straw-filled bed.

She squeaked in shock, but before she could sit back up he was on her, the wild expression in his eyes both terrifying and exhilarating. His fangs snapped out of his gums, and he groaned with relief before he buried his mouth in her breasts.

"No!" she gasped, bracing for the pain even as she grasped his hair to push him away from her flesh. But no sting of sharp teeth bit into her breast. He simply licked and sucked at the plump hills until his mouth closed around a stiff nipple in a cold embrace.

A groan she hadn't known she could produce escaped Thea as shocks of crackling pleasure shot through her. Her hands slipped from his hair and her head fell back on the bed while he sucked her nipple into an aching point.

Nimble fingers slipped between her thighs, ghosting cool touches along her smooth skin until they reached the tuft of hairs hiding her sex. Warin trailed a single digit up between her lower lips, parting her heated flesh and sending shivers of anticipation through her.

"You're so warm," he groaned into her heaving breasts, his mouth coming off her nipple with a wet pop. "So full of *life*." On that last hissed word, he shoved his questing finger deep, penetrating her slick cunny.

Thea gasped and arched off the bed, Warin's cool presence inside her setting her every nerve afire. He raised above her, his eyes alight with untamed yearning—for *her*. His beautiful face was twisted with desire, and those deadly fangs gleaming in the moonlight were a stark contrast to his angelic features. She knew she should fear him, fear his fangs and his desires alike, but every part of her only ached to unite her flesh with his.

When he curved his finger after a special place within, she lost the final shred of worry of what he was to the fire blast of raw pleasure burning through her writhing body.

"*Oh!* Warin! Yes! *More!*" Thea gripped him, every instinct within her aching to feel him, but he moved down between her spread legs before she could reach him... and put his mouth to her quivering heat.

The sensation of being kissed there, of feeling the flat

length of his fangs press up against her most sensitive flesh before his tongue delved in to part her, stole her breath away. She collapsed flat on the bed with a gasp, only to arch up high the next second when his cool lips closed around the little nub at the top of her cunny.

"Warin!" Her scream echoed through the room, hands flying to his tangled hair once more. Hard, deep, waves of pleasure rolled through her pelvis, so much stronger than anything she could ever find on her own. He was sucking it, she dimly realized, but too hard and too fast for any mortal to replicate, and all the while he rubbed his finger over the maddening spot deep inside her.

Her release came before she could prepare for it, tearing through her body in a molten burst that left her breathless and boneless on the straw-filled mattress.

She wasn't allowed a respite. The second her muscles released the vampire's finger, he moved above her quicker than her eyes could follow. When he pressed his cock between her still sopping folds, seeking entry with an impatient thrust of his hips, she cried out and clasped onto his strong shoulders in a feeble attempt at slowing his advances.

Warin growled, his body tense with obvious frustration, and when he finally stilled long enough to stare down at her, she saw his eyes were black like a predator's.

"Your body is ready, your moans say you are too... Why are you stopping me?" he demanded. The pressure against her opening didn't ease, but he wasn't forcing himself farther in, either.

"Go slow," she said, fighting back a smile at the frustration in his entire demeanor. It was pretty clear he'd never taken much care with his lovers before—but was trying his best with her, despite how desperate he was to be inside her. "If you go too fast, you'll hurt me."

He exhaled with a worried frown. Slowly, he eased down on one elbow. With his other hand he smoothed down the length of her thigh in a caress so gentle he may as well have touched her with a feather. Hungry eyes roamed over her skin, but he kept his touches soft and cautious.

"Touch me there again," she whispered, letting her own hand slide between their bodies to the nub of nerves he had made feel so good with his mouth.

Warin obeyed, brushing the back of his hand against her palm as he found her pleasure center with his thumb. The shock of bliss was immediate, and only intensified as he rubbed circles across the small pearl.

Thea groaned and tilted her hips up for more, inviting his thick cock inside as she did.

Careful this time, and without easing up on her clit, Warin put more pressure behind his hips. The delicious ache crested and was followed by an intense fullness that had Thea groaning and arching against him as he slid all the way inside. She may have lain with men before, but none had filled her so completely it bordered on pain.

Warin hissed above her, his fingers ripping deep grooves in the mattress as he clenched his hands in an obvious attempt at staying in control. But Thea no longer cared about the dull ache between her thighs as her insides spasmed fitfully around his intrusion. His cool flesh eased the pain of being opened wide to a delicious throb, and all she wanted in that moment was—

"*More!* Warin... give me *more!*" She wrapped her arms around his tense shoulders and pulled his body closer to hers. When he moved to follow her, rolling his hips with pained gentleness, ecstasy exploded in her blood. "Yes!" She raked her nails over his shoulders and wrapped her legs around the small of his back, needing him inside her more than she needed the air in her lungs.

A deep rumble tore from the vampire's chest, his eyes flaming at the sting of her nails, but despite the darkness she could see fighting to take control in his heated gaze, he kept the pace slow. Full, deep, rhythmic thrusts of his hips against hers drove her higher and higher, suspending her in an ocean of pleasure somewhere beyond reality.

And behind the sweet ecstasy of their physical union, there was something else. Something more. She *felt* his touch every time he bottomed out deep within her sheath, not simply in her body but also her soul. It was as if the core of her very being tried to reach out and embrace the monster between her thighs as tightly as her sex wrapped around his girth.

Soulmates, the witch had called them. Was that why being with him made her feel she was finally home? Finally whole?

Thea stared up at the vampire as he moved within her, eyes locked on hers and the deadly length of his fangs bared with the restraint he was exercising to keep their lovemaking gentle. Those fangs were the visceral proof of his inhumanity—of the monster she'd seen when they first met. But now... when she felt him so intimately, on every plane, as pleasure rushed through her veins... they were no longer a threat. They, and the hunger for blood she knew came with them, were what made him what he was —*who* he was. If he had been a man, they would never have found each other. He wouldn't have come to her village, wouldn't have sought her out.

In the final throes of passion, when her sex clenched around his cock and her release ripped through her body and mind, Thea knew she would have sacrificed her village a thousand times if it meant she would be with her soulmate in the end.

"Warin! Bite me!"

The vampire roared with relief, his eyes gleaming in the moonlight as he went for her throat, fangs piercing her skin and sinking deep into her flesh. The last thing she registered was a sharp sting in her neck and the cool rush of his seed deep inside. Then everything went dark.

CHAPTER 10

THEA

When Thea came to, the moon no longer shone through the small window, but Warin lay above her still as he lazily drew his tongue across her neck.

"Will I become like you?" she rasped. Both her cunny and voice were sore from the pleasure he'd forced from her, but much to her surprise, she didn't feel any pain where he'd bitten her.

"No," he said. His voice was soft now, so very different from how he'd sounded before. As if all his anger and fear had vanished when she shared her body with him. "A simple bite will not damn you, my beloved."

Beloved.

She smiled into the darkness. "I was so scared of you."

"I'm sorry." He sounded so guilty, she couldn't help but laugh.

"It seems silly now, doesn't it? That I could ever fear the man whose soul I share."

"I am not a man, and you were wise to fear me," he said, pulling back to look at her. She still couldn't make out his face in the darkness, but knew he likely didn't have such problems. "I am—"

"A monster," she interrupted him softly. "I know. It doesn't matter."

"The things I've done... Thea—"

She put her hand on his shoulder, silencing him with a light squeeze. "It doesn't matter. It can't. For whatever reason, and despite whatever we were before, we are one now. What you were before doesn't matter. What *I* was doesn't matter. I know you feel it too."

He sighed softly, an unnecessary breath that ghosted over her face. "I... feel such... shame. For tying you to... *this*. To me. I am of the night, and you... you are the brightest star in the sky. I fear... I will taint you."

"By sharing your curse with me?" she asked. A sliver of unease traveled up the length of her spine and she touched a hand to her neck where he had bitten her.

"No. *Never*. I will *never* turn you, my love. No one deserves this fate, least of all you."

"Then I will die," she said, remembering the frightening conversation between him and Zet. "I will grow old, and I will die. What will happen to you once I am gone?"

Just the thought of being without him made her insides turn to ice. The idea that he would have to go through that once her mortal body gave in hurt equally as bad. She couldn't imagine surviving losing him.

It had only been days since her only wish was to escape him, yet now...

Everything had changed.

"We have years until old age claims you," he said, though he held her tighter against his chest as if he subconsciously was already trying to prevent time itself from separating them. "I will find a way for us to be together in eternity, without dooming your soul to the darkness. When I rise tomorrow night, we will begin our travels to Rome. The Night Lady there may know more."

There were more questions she wanted to ask—things they had to discuss, plans they had to make... but Thea found she didn't have the will to do so. Not then. Even if there was no ward against old age, she didn't want to think about it now. He was right. They had years. Right now, she wanted nothing more than to lie in his embrace and savor the sated hum from deep inside the core of her being.

She found her soulmate. Nothing else mattered.

THE DARKNESS in the small room turned a deep gray before Warin roused her from her sleep by slipping out of the bed they'd shared.

"Where are you going?" she mumbled groggily as he bent to grasp his leather pants from the floor. Dawn was still nearly an hour away, but its pale march let her see his intricate tattoos move as his muscles flexed. They looked vaguely like the geometric figures she'd seen depicted on her village's attackers' shields, yet were different somehow.

"Dawn is near. I have to go underground until dusk." Warin turned to look at her, a gentle smile on his face she hadn't known his stark features could produce. He reached out and touched her cheek, and she pressed against his palm with an unhappy hum.

"I don't want you to go."

"I will return for you the second the sun sets," he promised softly. "Tonight, and every night after that, until the end of time."

"Where will you sleep?" she asked, frowning at the thought that he might have to leave the city during the day. She knew from the dirt caked on both his and Aleric's bodies that they dug graves to spend the day shielded from the sun. In the middle of a city, it seemed unlikely he would find somewhere hidden and undisturbed.

"The graveyard by the catacombs where Zet holds

court," he said. It was the first time he had shared his location during the daytime with her. The first time he trusted her enough to do so, she realized.

"The dead man sleeps in a graveyard," she mused. "I suppose that is poetic, in some way."

He didn't answer her—only leaned down to brush a gentle kiss to her lips.

"Tonight," she said as he walked to the door.

"Tonight," he confirmed. "And every night, my soulmate."

Sleep did not return to Thea after Warin left. She lay in bed, staring at the ceiling while night yielded for day. Thoughts seemed fleeting, the pleasant buzz in her body from their intimate time together drowning out any desire to think about the implications of their union.

It was not until sunlight filtered in through her small window that something caught the edges of her conscience. A niggling, as if someone was prodding her to gain her attention.

Thea frowned and sat up, unable to shake the sensation that someone *needed* her. It was the same sort of feeling she'd often had back in her village moments before someone would inevitably burst through her door in need of her healing herbs, the same sort of urgency.

Her eyes fell to the floor, and she frowned at the dark shadow outlined in the light from the window. When she looked up, she saw a large, black bird sitting outside the window, peering in. A raven, perhaps.

It looked like it was staring straight at her, and Thea fought a ridiculous impulse to cover her naked breasts. It was just a bird, after all. Even if...

The urgency coiling in her gut grew the longer she looked at the bird. It was almost as if... *it* wanted her help?

Thea drew in a deep breath as she slipped out of bed to find her clothes. She had lain with a Nightwalker and seen a witch light candles with a wave of her hand. A raven wanting her help wasn't the weirdest thing to have happened to her since she'd met Warin. Heck, it wasn't even the most outlandish thing that had happened in the past twelve hours.

The raven knocked its beak against the window, as if urging her to hurry.

"I'm coming, I'm coming," she muttered as she straightened her hair and brushed her hands over her dress. As quietly as she could so as not to disturb the other patrons, Thea let herself out of her room and tiptoed down the stairs.

The raven was waiting for her when she walked into the narrow street outside the inn. It gave a squawk at the sight of her and flew a couple of houses down, perching on a butcher's sign. Waiting for her. When she followed, it flew farther, leading the way through London's streets.

The sense of urgency in her gut grew as she stumbled along the cobbled roads, until finally, the raven dove into an alley so narrow the sun didn't touch its filthy depths.

Thea hesitated by the entrance as she tried to peer in through the darkness, but she couldn't see much of anything. The alley appeared to writhe like a serpent only a few yards in.

The raven squawked again from farther in. Calling her.

Thea stepped into the alley, letting the darkness swallow her up.

CHAPTER 11

WARIN

Consciousness snapped back into Warin's unmoving body with a pain so intense that for a moment, he thought someone had shoved a stake through his heart.

He gasped into the dark earth surrounding him on all sides, dazed and confused. He could still sense the presence of the sun in the sky. It was much too soon for him to rise, but the agony in his chest tore viciously at his body and roared through his mind.

Thea!

His soulmate's name echoed in his head and a wave of pure, unadulterated panic set in.

Thea. Something was wrong. She was…

It felt like a physical rending of his flesh, but it was his soul that ripped apart, shredded to pieces as the half of it he'd only found the previous night was torn away.

Warin bellowed and clawed at the dirt above him, but there was nothing he could do to get to his soulmate. He was trapped underground by the sun, imprisoned by his curse. He could do nothing but lie in the grave he'd invaded and wait for the sun's torturously slow crawl across the sky, praying to gods he no longer believed in that his soulmate was still among the living.

THE SECOND THE SUN SET, Warin burst from his grave. Damp soil crumbled from his body as he climbed up from the ground.

The crippling agony had long since died down to a dull pain lodged deep in his chest, icy numbness spreading in its place.

"What's going on?" Aleric asked. He was ascending from the grave next to Warin's, a clear note of worry in his voice. "I felt... *something* while I slept. In our bond?"

Warin didn't take the time to explain. He lifted his face to the dark sky and inhaled, scenting the air for any signs of his beloved. He found none.

Not caring if any human noticed his unnatural speed, he ran through the dark streets to the inn he'd left her at, hoping against hope she'd be there, waiting for him with that gentle smile on her lips.

"Ah, young sir!" the innkeeper greeted him when he burst in the door to the common room below. "Will you be needing the room another night, then?"

"Where is she?" Warin put the full force of his Compulsion behind his question. The innkeeper blinked dazedly.

"Your wife? She left with you this morning... didn't she?" the man said, his voice thick and sloppy from the strength of Warin's mind.

Warin didn't bother explaining—he sniffed the air and finally caught the faintest trace of Thea's scent. It was hours old.

He followed it outside where hundreds of people had soiled her crisp fragrance during the day, but something more than just his sense of smell guided him down the road. A pull from his chest led him through London's narrow streets, the sense of dread mounting in his gut for every yard he ran.

In the city's underbelly, the trail stopped without warning.

Warin faltered, looking around the cobbled path he was on. Houses rose on each side, and to his right a windy alleyway reeking of human waste opened up. The dread in his gut, rather than any remaining smell of his soulmate, made him step into the narrow opening. Even Thea's scent couldn't make it through the stench emanating from within.

He followed the alley along its coiling path until it opened up into a small, square space.

And in the center of the square lay his soulmate's lifeless body, her neck broken and sea-green eyes staring blindly into nothingness.

Pain so intense it made him stumble exploded behind his ribs as he stared at the woman he had loved so shortly.

"Thea! No!" Warin fell to his knees by her side. Crushing despair closed in around him from all sides.

"Thea! My love, no, no, no!" She was cold to his touch when he cradled her in his arms, her body stiff as if frozen by the shadows surrounding her while she lay in the alley, discarded like a piece of garbage. She had been dead for hours.

Deep down, he'd known the second he felt his soul splinter apart that she'd been ripped from him. Yet he had hoped with everything he was that he would find her alive. Injured, but alive.

But she was gone.

He'd only known her for a few days before she'd been torn from his side. Had only known the sweet bliss of *what* she was for mere hours.

She should have been his salvation.

"What happened?" Aleric asked, his concern and surprise vibrating through the alley.

Warin didn't pay him any mind. Tears of despair blinded him as he bit into his wrist and pressed the bloody limb to Thea's cold lips. He had sworn never to create another of their kind, but if he didn't... she would be lost to him forever. And he could never survive it.

CHAPTER 12
ALERIC

"What are you—?" Aleric caught himself as he stared in disbelief at his kneeling brother and the dead woman in his arms. It was obvious *what* he was trying to do—even if the *why* was less clear.

Cautiously, he crouched by Warin's side and put a hand on his shoulder. "Warin, she's been dead for hours. The spark won't catch."

"It will! It will, it has to! Come on, Thea. Please, come on, my love, I cannot... I cannot live without you!"

Aleric had never heard his Elder so distraught—the sheer panic in his voice and the raw pain in their bond sent waves of queasiness through him. If there was one thing Warin had always been, it was strong. Ruthless. Devoid of emotion except bloodlust. And now... now,

Warin was *sobbing*. Over a human girl who would have died soon enough regardless.

Aleric stared at his trembling brother as he tried to coax blood in between her long-dead lips, sick dread nestling deep in the pit of his stomach.

I cannot live without you.

Aleric's nausea turned to horror as he watched Warin kiss the dead girl's forehead, wrist still pressed to her mouth as tears slid down his pale cheeks. Finally, much too late, and with gut-wrenching clarity brought on by the sick pain echoing through their bond, Aleric realized what the loss of a soulmate did to a man.

It broke him.

"AH, the young Waldlitch brother returns for another night at my court. Do you care to join us for supper?"

Aleric glared at Zet as he made a sweeping motion with one arm toward a naked woman lying atop a sarcophagus, eyes wide with fear and chest heaving despite her complete stillness. She'd been Compelled to endure in silence as every vampire, save the Ancient himself, feasted on her blood dripping sluggishly from a multitude of bite marks.

"I wish to speak with you in private, *my lord.*" His

voice only narrowly avoided tipping into insubordination. "Urgently."

Zet raised an eyebrow at his tone. His second in command, the raven-haired Verawein, lifted her head from the human's weakly spasming wrist, undoubtedly in hopes of seeing her lord put a foolish youngling in his place, but the Ancient only sighed.

"Ah, the impatience of youth. Vera, my dear, if you would be so kind to deal with any urgent matters while I am gone?"

Verawein bowed her head, but Aleric didn't miss the calculating look she sent him as Zet turned to lead the way out of the catacomb where he held court.

This time, Zet didn't use the hidden exit, but walked along the same corridor his subjects used when entering his domain. He led Aleric to the ground floor of the church and into a modestly decorated chapel off the chancel, locking the door behind them.

The Ancient turned to Aleric, arms crossed over his chest. "Well?"

"You *killed* her!" Aleric hissed. "That was not part of the deal! Warin, he's... he's not himself. I fear he may end his life over this! Over that... *human!*"

"I distinctly remember how last we spoke, you worried the girl would get your brother killed, should she stay with him," Zet said softly. He lifted his hand to study his fingernails. "How he had changed since he came upon her, and no longer seemed to act rationally. I believe your exact words were: *'I would give much to have her vanish off the face of the Earth.'*"

Aleric gritted his teeth against the rage churning in his gut. He could still feel his Elder's distress echo through their bond in painful waves. "I didn't mean to fucking kill her!"

"Yes. You did." Zet finally looked up and straight at him, his golden eyes flaming with all the power of his age. His voice was no longer gentle. "You cannot lie to me, youngling. Were you truly so foolish to believe I let you drink from my witch out of the goodness of my heart? I know all your desires, Aleric. Every urge for power, and every shameful fear that that human girl would take your brother from you.

"I granted your wish. I eliminated what you perceived as a threat to your brother. So, tell me, why are you not groveling at my feet with gratitude? Could it be ridding Warin of his soulmate did not provide the outcome you desired?"

Aleric bared his teeth. Zet had his witch put a spell on him while he'd been busy reveling in the power of her blood. Of-fucking-course he had. Hadn't Warin warned him of the trickery of Ancients? And still, he'd been naive enough to accept the gift of magic-fueled blood from one, and had lowered his defenses enough to let a fucking witch put a spell on him.

He stared at the Ancient's smirk as he watched him much like a cat would eye its prey. Aleric had to be careful—he was already too entangled with this treacherous creature. But Warin needed help. He didn't know how much longer until his brother would realize the hopelessness in catching the spark of a several hours old corpse. And once he did...

"Please, my lord. My brother requires help. I know we are not of your territory and you have limited obligations toward outsiders, but you are the only Ancient on the Isles."

Zet stared, unblinking. "His soulmate is dead, Aleric. I may be powerful, but even I cannot undo this. What do you wish for me to do to aid your brother? I cannot turn back time."

"Your witch—she is strong," Aleric said quickly, desperation fueling him. "I've heard stories... Can she—"

Zet lifted a hand, interrupting him with a dark eyebrow arched in disbelief. "Can she animate the corpse of your brother's beloved? No, youngling, I am not so foolish as to keep a witch with that kind of power alive. Besides... even if such a witch could be procured, it would be for naught. She would only animate flesh and bones—the girl's soul is gone."

Aleric clenched his fists, wracking his brain for an answer. There had to be a way. He couldn't lose Warin—not now, not ever. His desire to secure his Elder's undead life was why he'd wished the fucking human gone in the first place. "If your witch cannot bring the human to life, can she make him forget? If he can't remember her, he can't miss her."

It was the deepest betrayal. He knew that. Asking a witch to put a curse on his blood brother—if Warin ever learned of his desperate request, he would tear him limb from limb. But if it could save his life, Aleric didn't care.

Zet looked intrigued. He cocked his head as he regarded Aleric, golden eyes narrowed. "Now *that*... That might be possible. But there will be a cost. Are you certain you wish to add another favor to what you already owe me? I do not take debts lightly, and I *will* collect."

Add a debt to a favor he'd not been asked. Aleric gritted his teeth. He had no choice—the Ancient had played him into a corner. If he rebelled against his demands, Warin would die.

Aleric bent his head in submission. Clenching his fists until his knuckles whitened, he said, "Yes, my lord. I am certain. Help me ensure Warin lives, and I will gladly repay any debt you wish to claim from me."

THE WITCH LAY motionless on the bed when they entered her darkened room, but at the sound of their entry, her eyelids flickered open.

"Twice in as many nights?" she murmured. "Has ruling lost its appeal, my lord, since you seek out my company over your loyal subjects'?"

"While your delights certainly are intriguing, little dove, I am not here for my own entertainment. I believe you may recall our friend from last night?" Zet asked as he motioned for Aleric to step forward.

Marie sat up, her dark eyes roaming over Aleric's frame with a not entirely hostile gleam. Had he not been so desperate to save Warin before he lost his mind to sorrow, he would likely have returned her interest. As with most vampires, his feedings were usually followed by other desires, and witch blood had proven potent in more than one way. By the time they were done, Marie had seemingly forgiven her Master for forcing her to tell Warin what Thea was.

"Back for seconds?" the witch purred, tilting her neck back in teasing invitation.

"Our friend is in need of your help. He wants to know if you can alter memories," Zet said, seemingly unfazed by the swell of her breasts and her creamy neck.

Marie's expression soured. "Our arrangement was not

for you to sell my abilities for your own gain, Zet. I'm not a common whore."

The Ancient gave her a small smile. He crossed the floor and gracefully sat on the bed next to her, grasping her jaw with one hand. When he turned her face to his, there was iron in his gaze. "Our *arrangement* is that you offer your body, your blood, *and* your abilities whenever I demand, and in return, I let you live. You *are* a whore, Marie, and I am your master. I suggest you remember this if you do not wish for me to withhold my blood again."

The witch paled, eyes widening. "P-please, my lord, I'm sorry. Please. I'll die without your blood."

"Painfully so," he murmured, brushing her hair away from her neck in a caress, his ire obviously calmed at her swift submission. "Now, tell me... can you help our friend?"

She nodded, gaze downcast. "It is... very tricky, but it's possible."

"What are we waiting for, then? Let's get started," Aleric said. "I need you to remove Warin's memories of his soulmate. Every last one."

Marie looked up at him, a small smile on her lips. "Is that's what this is about? You think just erasing his memories will heal his soul? It's been rent in two, vampire. He is lost. Forever."

So she knew Thea was dead. Aleric glanced at Zet,

but his expression betrayed nothing. Not that it mattered if she'd been involved in the Ancient's scheme—she was nothing more than a slave to her master's wishes.

"Make him forget her," Aleric said, steel in his voice. "He was whole before her, he will be whole after as well. Tell me what you need and make it happen. We don't have much time."

"Blood," she said. "I need his blood. Or yours."

Of-fucking-course. It always came back to the blood. Aleric stalked across the room, rolled up his sleeve, and bit into his own wrist. Crimson drops pooled at the edges of the wound and threatened to drip on the floor. Before they could, Marie fetched a chalice from the small table and caught the blood. She collected every drop that leaked from his wrist until the wound closed over, leaving only smooth skin behind.

The witch carried the chalice to the end of the bed where a small trunk sat. Kneeling in front of it, she opened it and rummaged through its depths to retrieve several dried herbs.

"Come." She motioned at Aleric as she got to her feet.

He went to her, ignoring the small hairs at the back of his neck standing on end as invisible power gathered around the witch. Once he was by her side, she gave him a cold smile and whispered, *"Protega."*

Flames sprang up around them in a perfect circles,

sparking green magic as they hissed against the uneven floorboards.

Marie drizzled the dried herbs into the chalice, muttering incantations until it began to bubble. When emerald sparks flew from the cup, she downed the viscous liquid in one long gulp, threw the chalice to the floor, and lifted her hands. Verdant light shone from them as she reached up to clasp her palms to each side of Aleric's face. He felt the sear of her magic and smelled the stench of it as he stared into her dark eyes.

Everything in him ached to snap her neck and drain her lifeblood to end the threat of her power, but he fought himself to stay still. Whatever he had to withstand to ensure Warin forgot about Thea, he would. Even allowing a witch to use him for her foul magic.

"Look at me," Marie snapped. "Allow my magic into your blood, vampire. Welcome it. Can you feel it? Can you feel it filling you? Searching... Think about the girl. Picture her with him."

Aleric obeyed, his mind searching for every time he had seen the two of them together. The look of wonder and frustration in his brother's eyes. Her fear. They should never have met—this soulmate shit was an abomination. Whatever Fate had planned, it had been wrong. His brother was strong, fierce... a warrior to the bone. No human female would ever tie him down, not even in death.

He felt the moment Marie's magic connected with his memories. It sparked through his blood in unpleasant shocks, but he gritted his teeth and endured. As he would endure anything for Warin. Even the act of betrayal.

"He has forgotten her," the witch said, staring into his eyes. "He no longer remembers her face, nor his shared time with her. She will be forever wiped from his memory, from now until the end of time. Swear by the blood that this is what you desire."

"I swear it. By the blood, I swear this is my desire."

His veins burned sharply in response, making him cry out. It was gone as quickly as it came, leaving him shaking in the witch's grasp.

She smiled that same cool smile at him and lowered her palms from his face. The flames died down, leaving only a singed circle around them. Echos of power still vibrated through the room, but quieted for every shuddering, unnecessary breath Aleric drew to calm his mind.

"It is done," Marie said, stepping back from him. "He will not recognize her if he sees her again."

"Sees her again?" Aleric asked as he worked his shoulders. His body still felt stiff from the invading magic. "She's dead."

The witch shook her head at him as if he were a slow child. "Some souls reincarnate. We do not know which, but even if hers does... he will not know her. She could pass him on the street and he would never see her for what she truly is."

"Thorough. I like it," Aleric said with a short nod. The last thing he needed was to go through all this shit and end up in an Ancient's debt just to have Thea pop up again in a few decades. "I believe our business here is done. My lord, I trust you have your methods of finding me when you wish to have my debt made good." He nodded at Zet as he rolled his sleeve back down and stalked toward the door, more than ready to find Warin and get the hell out of London.

"There is one more thing," the witch called from behind him. He paused, though he wanted nothing more than to keep walking until he would never have to see her or this cursed room again.

"The spell is thorough. It won't just work on your brother. No vampire in your bloodline, whether they walk the Earth today or in several hundred years, will recognize his soulmate, should he come across her." Her voice rang with smug satisfaction. "You will not curse any more of my sisters with your tainted souls."

CHAPTER 13
ALERIC

It didn't take Aleric long to find Warin. He was wandering the streets nearby where they had discovered Thea's corpse. Aleric followed the now oddly muted pull from their bond, weaving through drunks and late night revelers until he finally laid eyes on his brother.

The absence of violent pain in their bond spoke the truth of the witch's words—her spell had worked.

Aleric couldn't care less if he never found some human girl to fuck with his mind like Thea had with Warin. Marie's revelation that she'd cursed their entire bloodline seemed more like a blessing. He had no interest in losing himself like Warin nearly had. No, if the witch had ensured neither of them would ever suffer this *soul-mate* bullshit ever again, perhaps the visit to London had been worth it after all. Even if he had no doubts Zet would call on him to fulfill his debt at some point in the future.

"Brother!" He called out at the sight of Warin's slumped form resting against a building. He walked to his side at human pace, fighting the urge to use his supernatural speed to get to him quicker, and clasped a hand to his shoulder. "Have you fed? Are you ready to leave this hellhole of a town? I can't wait to get as far away from any and all Ancients as we possibly can!"

Warin slowly turned his head toward him, his blank face devoid of the usual zest for life that had adorned it since the day they escaped to the wilds together. "I am not hungry. We can leave if you wish."

Aleric frowned at the apathy in his brother's voice. Warin's usually vibrant blue eyes were flat, deadened. It struck him that, despite their undead state, he had never seen his brother so devoid of life, as if he truly was nothing more than a walking corpse.

You think just erasing his memories will heal his soul? It's been rent in two, vampire. He is lost. Forever.

The witch's words rang through his mind as he stared at the husk of the man he'd known and loved all his undead life, sick dread burning in his gut.

Warin seemed to notice his stare and smiled softly. "What has you so worried, brother? Tell me you didn't bed the Ancient's bonded human, or something equally Aleric-like."

Relief flooded through Aleric. He returned Warin's smile with a grin and squeezed his shoulder. "Would I do something like that? All I'm saying is we should probably get out of town before dawn."

His brother would be all right. It might take him some time to heal from the impact of such a strong spell, but he would pull through.

One month of hunting through the deep forests of the continent and no remnants of Thea's curse would be left from their time on the Isles.

No *soulmate* would break his wild brother.

EPILOGUE
WARIN

2017 - Chicago, IL.

"There has been another disappearance."

Warin sighed as he put the pen down on top of the pile of paperwork stacked neatly on his desk.

"Who?" He lifted his gaze to look at his second in command.

The woman walked closer to his desk and placed a folder on top of his other paperwork. "A youngling. His Sire says he felt their bond die last night."

Warin flicked the folder open. A photograph of a blond young man stared back at him. His cocky smile reminded Warin of Aleric and a wave of unexpected sadness washed through him. He hadn't felt much of anything for a long while, he realized. Not since he and

Aleric parted ways more than three decades ago, once his brother also reached the status of an Ancient.

Having two such powerful beings within the same territory for any length of time had a way of upsetting the fragile balance within the vampire community, so Aleric had been forced to leave his side. He now ruled the territory of Denver and the surrounding areas. A strong territory for such a relatively new Ancient, but he wasn't surprised. Aleric had matured into a shrewd politician in the past few centuries, some of his attention turning from women and battle to intrigues and political plots. He'd even had a not insignificant part in the War for Independence back in the eighteenth century, and again during the Night of Revelations in the 1970s.

How long had it been since they even spoke?

Warin stared at the photograph of the youngling and wondered if his Sire would Embrace a new Child, or if the wound left behind from their broken bond would drive him to insanity. If it did, it would be Warin's job to give him his Final Death. He'd had to do it once before in his capacity as Night Lord of Chicago and the surrounding areas. A Sire lost her Child and lover and went on a rampage through central Chicago that'd nearly gotten the humans' army called in.

This new disappearance was the third in his territory within the span of six months.

"I will tell the Guard to find those responsible and punish them accordingly," his second said, motioning toward the folder to retrieve it.

"No." Warin closed it, hiding the smiling youngling from view. "The Guard has failed me enough. If these disappearances keep happening, then clearly they have not gotten to the root of the problem."

"My lord—"

"*I* will deal with it. Personally." He stood up, fingertips resting lightly on the mountains of paperwork that had kept him behind his desk for the past many months. Years, if he were to be truly honest. It had been years since he had so much as visited his own city. Not since he'd had to kill that grieving Sire.

"I... as you wish," his second said, bowing her head. "How long will you be gone?"

"As long as it takes. I am certain Chicago will be in good hands under your watch."

And, Warin thought as he slipped out of the stately mansion where he kept his small court, if he ended up not returning, perhaps she would be the one to show the youngling's Sire his Final Death. She was older than most of their kind at just over six hundred years. She would be able to handle the responsibilities that came with his position for as long as she needed to.

He was duty bound to find the culprit for these disappearances—they had happened under his watch. But after that... maybe it was time that he, too, disappeared. Aleric was an Ancient now with responsibilities of his own. Once he put an end to the disappearances, there would be no more obligations left. No more reason to continue an existence that had had little to do with living for the past many centuries.

Warin left the quiet suburban neighborhood that unwittingly had hosted his nest for more than a decade, deciding to investigate the place of the youngling's disappearance on foot while avoiding the attention a car would draw. The humid air felt pleasant against his skin, and for a moment he wished he was barefoot—like he had been many centuries ago when he and Aleric would roam the wild forests of Europe.

HE DIDN'T NOTICE the raven perched on the phone wire outside his front gates, watching him disappear into the night.

WICKED SOUL

ANCIENT BLOOD: ONE

Warin's story continues in book 1 of the *Ancient Blood* series: *Wicked Soul.*

__He saved me… And then he blood-bonded me.__
__Now I'm his.__

My first meeting with a Chicago vampire went better than expected.

Up until that night, all I knew about vampires was limited to a few common facts: they drink blood, they get a mean sunburn and if you find yourself alone with one, you're dead.

Except he didn't kill me.

Sexy, broody Warin clearly had his own reasons for sparing my life and tying me with his blood, but if he'd known how much trouble I'd attract, I bet he wouldn't have bothered. When he blood-bonded me, secrets even I didn't know about myself came to light.

Secrets that will pull us both deep into the eternal war between vampires and the witches determined to rid the world of their evil.

We have only one choice now: fight the forces hell-bent on breaking our bond...

Or die.

"*Ow*, what's *wrong* with you?" I aimed a futile kick at the burly guy manhandling me out of the back of the white van he'd tossed me in a good twenty minutes earlier.

A smarter girl would probably have been terrified at being kidnapped off the street, but I was mainly just furious.

"Let go of me, you goddamn fanatic!"

Then again, most girls didn't get tossed into the back of cross-riddled vans for their choice in reading material. Somehow, even as the big goon wrenched my bound hands up high behind my back and shoved me through the door of a house somewhere in the bad part of Chicago's suburbs, part of me still thought it was all some horrible joke. Any minute now, an over-excited TV host would jump out with a bunch of cameras and tell me I'd been pranked. *Haha.*

I looked around the inside of the house. There wasn't any light apart from the little that managed to seep in through the dirty windows, but from what I could see of the room we were in, no one had lived here for a very long time. There was no furniture, apart from a broken couch and a tipped-over coffee table in the far corner of the room, and both walls and flooring looked like they were rotting away.

"Time to learn what happens to filthy little vamp sluts," the guy who'd been driving the van sneered as he closed the door behind us.

"Jesus, the state of public education is as bad as the Internet says, huh? I swear to you, reading a paranormal romance novel is not the same as *actually* banging a vampire."

Yup, that was what had gotten me kidnapped

Reading a sexy vampire book at a cafe, minding my own business. I swear, this sort of thing could only happen to me.

"Shut your mouth, bitch," the goon behind me growled, giving me a hard shove that had me stumbling across the floor and face-planting against a heavy, wooden door. "Don't you dare take the Lord's name in vain!"

Okay, so not a game show then. I swallowed a

whimper of pain when he yanked me away from the door by a grip on my ponytail so he could unlock and open it.

I was pretty sure, despite the sorry state of American TV these days, that no candid camera would get away with physically abusing its unsuspecting contestants. The acrid taste of true fear burned in my throat when realization of how bad my situation truly was finally set in.

I gritted my teeth against the swell of panic in my chest when the newly opened door revealed a dark, narrow staircase leading down below ground level. I tried to throw myself back and away from the gaping chasm of darkness in front of me, but it was useless. My kidnappers simply gave me a shove between the shoulder blades, and thanks to my bound wrists, I didn't have any means of resisting.

Squealing, I stumbled down the stairs, only narrowly managing to keep on my feet, until I smacked up against another door, this one made of solid metal. Face first. Again.

The goon and his accomplice were right behind me, and a second later, I was shoved through yet another door. Pale light illuminated the walls of a large, concrete room. I stared open-mouthed at the many odd-looking weapons lining the walls—wooden stakes, crossbows, scary-looking knives. And among them, crosses and long metal chains of varying thicknesses. Just what the hell sort of place was this?

"The sun sets in two hours, deadwhore. If I were you, I'd spend that time praying for forgiveness," my kidnapper sneered. He pulled a knife and sliced through the zip-ties binding my wrists, then pointed at the far end of the room. "Get in."

I followed his finger with my eyes and saw a large, metal cage half-hidden behind a pile of junk. *Whoa, whoa, whoa.* Who the fuck had a cage in their basement? Just how many girls did they force into their little rape-cave because of their taste in smutty literature?

My frozen silence was met with a gentle, yet unmistakably threatening poke of a knife's point against the back of my neck.

"In."

Slowly, I forced my feet to move toward the cage where the other guy was holding the cell door open for me. *How fucking gallant.*

I glared at him as he swung the gate shut with a clang, locking it behind me and taking a step back.

"How long do you plan on keeping me in here?" I demanded, feeling oddly relieved to have bars between us. It was an illusion of safety, of course, since they held the keys, but it was enough for me to find some of my anger again. And anger felt a lot better than fear.

"Oh, just for a couple of hours," the driver said, a cruel smirk on his face. "If you get bored, you can always see if you can wake up your new friend."

He nodded at something behind me, and I turned halfway around to see what the hell the crazy old goat was referring to.

And that was when I realized I wasn't alone in the cage.

A dark-haired young man who looked like he was in his early twenties sat cross-legged at the back of the cage on the bare concrete floor. His eyes were closed and he wasn't moving a muscle, a serene look on his face as if he was meditating or something.

Outraged, I spun back around to my kidnappers. "Great, so now you kidnap college kids? What did he do, watch *Van Helsing*? You sick fucks!"

Both men laughed, and I felt like I was missing some twisted joke. "Start begging God for forgiveness. You don't have much time left."

"What the hell is that supposed to mean?" I snapped, but they didn't answer me. Instead they turned around and left the room, the heavy metal door closing behind them. The keys rattled in the lock from the other side, and then I was alone with the meditating college kid.

I cussed and turned around, leaning heavily against the metal bars. What the hell sort of crazy wackjobs kidnapped people off the streets and locked them in their creepy basement?

I looked at the kid—or guy. A possibly twenty-one-year-old would likely take umbrage with being called a kid.

He still hadn't so much as cracked open an eyelid at the commotion of getting a new cellmate.

I pinched my lips in a disapproving frown. Nice to see that *someone* could keep their cool while being locked up by crazies. "Hey, hello?"

Not even a muscle spasm to indicate he'd heard me.

Was he in some sort of trance? Or was he just a complete asshole? I knelt down on the concrete in front of him so my face was less than five inches from his and stared intently at him. "Hello?"

Still no response.

I blew in his face. Perhaps not the most mature thing I could have done, but his complete lack of interest in my existence was just the tipping point. I'd just been kidnapped and manhandled, and he couldn't even take a break from being all hipster-zen? Hello, damsel in distress here!

A groan slipped past his full lips as he opened a single eye to a narrow slit.

"Don't... do that." It was hardly more than a whisper, and his eyelid immediately closed again.

His obvious grogginess scared me. Was he sick? Drugged? Just what on earth had they done to him?

"Are you all right?" My voice pitched shrilly with worry, all thoughts about my own shitty situation vanishing. When he didn't respond, I slapped him across the face and gently shook his shoulders with both hands to make sure he didn't slip into unconsciousness. "You gotta stay with me, okay?"

Slowly, both his eyelids cracked open this time, revealing nearly black eyes with just a ring of blue, so much were his pupils blown.

"Shh, little one." He slowly lifted a hand from his knee and wrapped it loosely around my right wrist. Gently, he pried my hand off his shoulder before he let go again, his hand falling bonelessly back down in his lap. "Have to sleep... a little longer. Until... sunset."

Bewildered, I moved back a little so I wasn't breathing right in his face, but I stayed in my low crouch so I could study his blank features for clues. His hand had been very cold against my skin, and even though we were in a basement, it worried me. He clearly wasn't feeling well, and just what was everyone's obsession with sunset around here?

His pale face and the fact that he was hardly breathing made me worry he was seriously, fatally ill, and

I somehow doubted the creeps who had locked us both in this cage would care to call an ambulance.

I rubbed my face in frustration and tried to recall what I'd learned about caring for possibly-dying people on my one and only first aid course nearly eight years ago. It was then that I realized he wasn't breathing at all.

"Omigoddess!" My pulse sped up to warp-speed as adrenaline kicked in, but it turned out my instincts were on point even if most of my conscious brain was busy freaking out.

With a swifter movement than was usual for me, I tackled my cellmate to the ground and pinched his nose shut before I put my lips on his and blew air into his lungs.

This time, his eyes opened wide as a cough shuddered through his body.

"Oh, thank the stars!" I gasped as I placed a hand on his chest, relieved beyond belief to feel his chest moving again. "You stopped breathing! You..."

But his chest *wasn't* moving.

I glanced from my hand against his completely still torso to his face. His eyes were still open, looking at me as if he couldn't quite comprehend that a stranger had just tried to perform CPR on him.

But he wasn't breathing.

And his heart wasn't beating, either.

It was in that moment that my brain finally decided to arrive at the party.

Sleeps until sundown, cold to the touch, doesn't breathe...

"Motherfucking *fuck!*" I flew backward and scrambled away from him until the bars at the other end of the cage pressed against my back, unable to take my eyes off his still form even as his eyes slid shut again.

Mother above!

I was locked in a cage with a... a *vampire!*

DARKNESS

Into the Darkness

Hidden in Darkness

Shades of Darkness

Fires in the Darkness

MADE & BROKEN

Dangerous

Monster

Trouble